THEY SAY LOVE IS BLIND
PEPPER PACE

An IR Novella

THEY SAY LOVE IS BLIND

PEPPER PACE

They Say Love is Blind

REVIEWS FOR THEY SAY LOVE IS BLIND

I still shake my head because I passed over her books thinking they would be more tragic. I was so wrong because this is romance written at its best.
-Dharp; APB Perspective Reviews

I really enjoyed this story that emphasizes love really is blind and I'll definitely read more from this author.
-Shelly; Red Hot Books, blog

Ms. Pace has created yet another compelling couple in Lee and Tory.
-Theodora Taylor; Interracial Romance Book Reviews

They Say Love is Blind

They Say Love is Blind

Cover art created by Kim Chamber

FORWARD

I have countless versions of this story, created in the attempt to tweak and perfect the beautiful couple described here. Those of you that are familiar with my work may remember one such version of this story that appeared on Literotica.com.

I am often asked if the story that appeared in print 'for free' is the same story that is being sold. The answer to that is absolutely not. While the characters and storyline will remain true to the online/free version, you will find that my stories are completely re-edited when submitted for publishing. In this particular story it has tripled in size, which means that the characters are exploring situations never presented in any other version of this story.

With that said, I hope you enjoy Tory and Lee's journey to love.

-Pepper Pace

ACKNOWLEDGMENT

I must thank Hugo Morais for his contribution to the editing of this story. Being Azorean, Hugo was able to give me wonderful insight into the lifestyle and language of these beautiful people. It is due to his wonderful insight that I was able to put a breath of realism into this tale.

Table of Contents

CHAPTER 1

It seemed like every day Tory was late for work. She'd already missed the first bus and was about to miss the late bus. She called the second bus the late bus because no matter what, she was destined to walk in to the office at least one minute late. But at least if she was only one or two minutes late it meant that she might be able to slip in unnoticed.

She saw the bus rounding the corner and was forced to break into a run. Her neatly pressed hair was going to end up a mass of nappy curls.

Tory sprinted, hoping not to twist an ankle, trying not to think about how embarrassing she must appear to the other commuters. She wasn't exactly small but despite her extra weight she moved with a speed born of desperation and managed to reach the bus before it pulled off.

Breathlessly she searched for change and then almost fell when the driver began to take off before she was settled. She was forced to sit down in the handicap, elderly section so that she could dig through her oversized purse for her wallet. Her purse doubled as a lunch bag, overnight bag, and sometimes even a trash bag. It held everything

1

from a doo-rag, old bills, a snack cake to a bottle of hairspray.

"Do you need change?" A man's quiet voice asked.

"No," she said absently, trying to catch her breath. "It's just all over my bag-" Finally she came up with the coins. She stood up and reached for the pole, but the bus took that particular opportunity to lurch forward and Tory lost her balance before she could grab hold. She found herself falling into the lap of the man who had offered the change.

"Oh!" His hand came up reflexively to her ample hips. She leaped up. "I am so sorry!" This was a day from hell. She heard the snickers of several commuters. She was really putting on a show today. She felt embarrassed beads of sweat sprout under her arms.

"It's okay," the man replied facing forward stiffly. He did reach down to retrieve her sweater. He handed it up to her absently still without looking at her. She flushed realizing that she must have embarrassed him too, and bearing all of her weight might have even injured him.

"Thank you. Sorry again," she murmured then paid her fare and hurried to the rear of the bus.

If she could, she would have sank into her seat and turned into plastic. No wonder most people wore running shoes until they actually got into the office. It wasn't that she was trying to be cute or anything, she literally had no time to lace up running shoes.

Tory peeked up to the front of the bus at the man she'd become unintentionally familiar with. He was a good-looking white man with short hair. It curled despite the fact that it was only about an inch in length. Brown hair matched his olive skin; Italian, maybe? Well he was fine as hell. Not that many white guys appeared this early in the bus ride. Usually the whites didn't appear until the bus moved closer to the center of town where there were more white-collar jobs and the shopping was more upscale. Her neighborhood was definitely more Urban, though not a bad part of town. No, Tory had a nice apartment on a nice, predominantly black street.

Her face felt hot. Why did she have to fall into a white man's lap?! He continued to stare forward watching the scenery go by, though he had relaxed now that she wasn't assaulting his lap. She dug into her purse again, this time for a mirror. She examined her makeup and gasped.

"My God…" Her hair had dropped and her makeup was a shiny runny mess. She dabbed at her face with a tissue and then ended up pinning her long hair into a French twist. A while later when she looked up again, the handsome man was gone.

That night after Tory returned home from work, she swore to herself that she was going to be out of the apartment at a decent hour from here on out. She dug into the freezer for a Lean Cuisine meal to pop into the microwave. She was starving! The diet she was on wasn't going very well. At work today, everything had been fine through her first break, through lunch, until last break when she felt compelled to stop at Starbucks for a simple cup of coffee and ended up with a Venti Malt Frappucino and slice of chocolate chip cheesecake...

Tory sighed and slipped off her clothes as her meal heated. She unhooked her bra allowing her heavy breast to flop out. She scratched in pleasure that the torture device was off. She hated her breast and her belly, her hips, her butt...because all of those things were big. After work she had gone to check out a new gym, which was on her bus route. She figured that she could give the gym an hour of her time in the evenings. But when she looked at the sweating bodies fear overwhelmed her and she left before a sales person could pressure her into purchasing a membership that she'd never use.

She slipped on a nightshirt and furry slippers and then settled down in front of the T.V. set with her meal and a diet coke. Maybe she'd start Atkins again. She'd lost on Atkins...

Tory woke with a start, unsure of where she was. And with a jolt she realized that she'd fallen asleep in front of the television.

"Oh NO!" She looked at the clock. It was the next morning and she was going to miss her bus! She leaped to her feet sprinting to the bathroom where she jumped into the shower and washed quickly. Her hair was ruined so she just pulled it back into a bun. Not completely dry, she pulled on underwear, a simple loose dress and black mules. Then she ran out of the apartment and down the street to catch the late bus.

She alternated between cursing, praying and begging. Tory had a tardiness problem, which meant she could get away with a minute or two late but more than that would be documented. She rounded the corner just as the bus was approaching the stop. She had to be the laughing stock of the day for the other commuters: fat girl running after the bus every day. She breathlessly boarded, hearing someone giggle. She frowned at the obnoxious woman sitting in the elderly handicapped area. She looked like she had just left her job as a pole dancer. She was smirking at Tory who concentrated on making sure to grip the pole and plant her feet so that when the driver took off he wouldn't topple her.

She had a sneaking suspicion that the bus driver enjoyed watching her lose her balance. This time instead of trying to find change, she just slipped in two dollar bills, and then sank into the handicap, elderly seat until she could safely make her way to the back of the bus.

The man from yesterday was there sitting right next to her.

"Good morning," she spoke politely, still trying to catch her breath.

"Good morning," he replied. His husky deep voice sent chills down her spine. Something about it was very sexy.

"Sorry again about yesterday." He didn't reply but his lips curled into a slight smile of amusement. The bus came to a stop and Tory quickly gripped her belongings and hurried to her normal seat at the rear of the bus. When she was settled in her seat she didn't bother to check the mirror. She already knew how she'd look. She peeked at the man, not wanting to get caught staring, but he was hard not to look at.

Again, he watched the scenery as it passed with no interest in the other commuters. She tried to imagine what a man like that did for a living. She did it with everyone that rode the bus as a way to pass the time. Mr. Cutie didn't wear a suit, or uniform. He wasn't a construction worker; he was dressed too nice for that, but maybe an electrician, or computer tech? Her eyes scanned his clothing. He wore Dockers and a black long sleeved pullover Henley. That didn't really tell her much, other than that he had a nice, lean body, and that he might change into something else once he got to his destination.

Oh well, she enjoyed watching and the fantasies that she could come up with wouldn't be bad either. But as usual, fantasies were all that she ever had with the good-looking guys...or any guys for that matter. Tory hadn't been on a date in years and she barely knew what it was to be kissed. She wasn't a virgin because she was insecure about her looks, or because no one wanted to have sex with her. Tory was a virgin because she wouldn't allow the fact that someone had taken her innocence forcibly to dictate when she'd 'actually' lose her virginity. And until she met the 'right' person a born again virgin is what she'd remain.

It wasn't a horrible existence. The internet afforded her with a sexual outlet. But she was pretty sure that if she ever needed repair work done on her computer she'd just trash it and buy a new one. She'd just have to be satisfied with watching from afar; the story of her life.

She turned back to the front of the bus in time to see his curly head disappearing out the door. She strained to see him out of one of the windows but she was on the wrong side of the bus and the driver took off entirely too fast. Oh well, it was kinda pathetic anyway, that just watching a good looking guy from afar would be the high point of her day.

While at work she overheard two of her co-workers rave about a Portuguese restaurant not too far off of her bus route. She had never eaten Portuguese and couldn't imagine what kind of food would be served there, but listening to the two women talking really intrigued her. Her love of new food is what had packed on the pounds in the first place. But eating out was her only form of entertainment. Tory knew that if she weren't always on a diet she'd be a true foodie. Her perfect life would be a fat, happy foodie with a boyfriend who loved trying new things as much as she did.

So that evening after work, Tory decided to treat herself to dinner out. The thought of eating another Lean Cuisine meal was nauseating and if she ate another piece of microwave chicken she was going to grow feathers!

Since The Jewel of the Azores Restaurant was not too far from her home, Tory stayed on the bus and bypassed her usual stop until she reached the section of town where all of the trendy restaurants sprouted. It was a melting pot where people from all over the world converged. She loved staring at the people each time she had to travel through this section of town and thought that it would be

8

awesome to one day explore it. Now she would get the chance.

After she determined the correct stop, Tory had no choice but to walk the 8 blocks from the bus stop to the restaurant, seldom did she look forward to walking but when street performers and strange shops lined the streets and live music could be heard how could she not enjoy it? Luckily she was wearing flats today. Perhaps she'd burn a couple of calories before she replaced them with Portuguese food--whatever that might be.

Eventually she hobbled into the restaurant. Her shins felt like someone had kicked them and her chest was on fire.

The hostess stepped back when she came in panting. "Um...how many?" She asked with a concerned look on her face.

"O-one." Tory managed while leaning against a heavy wooden post trying to catch her breath.

"Follow me." Tory noted the couples and families crowding the small establishment. It was obviously popular. The smells sent Tory's mouth watering. She was shown a small table off to a corner. She had long ago given up her discomfort of eating alone. At the age of 27 Tory was used to doing everything alone. It wasn't that she didn't have friends. But they had boyfriends or families.

She opened the menu and read a brief introduction about the Azores; she didn't even realize there was such a place. The owners were smart to show pictures of the various dishes because the names were strange. Written in Portuguese, the titles were long and impossible for her to bend her tongue around. There was everything on the menu from seafood and blood sausage to tripe and stew.

She grinned. This is exactly what she liked; a new experience. A pretty waitress came to her table. She looked like she enjoyed food as much as Tory did and so Tory asked her to recommend something.

"We have a fishermen's stew which has whitefish, white beans within a tomato stock. We have a Portuguese chicken which is mildly spicy, has rice, cheese and stewed in a tomato stock-"

Tory watched the young woman intently as she rattled off the popular items. "But what do YOU like?"

The waitress paused and allowed her eyes to linger on Tory. She smiled in a more relaxed manner. "My favorite dish is definitely *sopa de couves*."

Tory was nodding her head. She had no idea what that was. "I'll have that please."

The waitress gave her one nod. "And to drink?"

Tory passed her menu to the waitress. "I'll let you decide."

The woman retreated with the menu and Tory took in her surroundings in more detail, admiring the mural on the wall of an Island with palm trees and people looking suntanned and happy. Soft music played something that sounded like a strange jazz and Spanish fusion. The room was painted in vibrant tones and colorful pieces of art dotted the walls. It was trendy yet comfortable. There was even a bar that looked like a tiki hut-

Tory froze, heartbeat lurching in a jolt of surprise. Her eyes scanned the familiar profile, the short hair with the promise of curls, the tanned skin and the light brown eyes. It was the cutie from the bus! He was enjoying a meal at the bar and he was alone, too. Tory felt a warm flush of excitement. Imagine that...

As she sat staring at him from across the room, a woman approached him. Ahh, so he was waiting for his woman. He'd started eating without her but she didn't look like she ate anyways. Tory wasn't surprised to see that his woman had a body that should dance in rap videos and a face that would rival Halle Berry's. So he liked black women? Well who would care about race when your woman looked like that!

The woman took the stool next to him and began talking. He began shaking his head and said a few words before turning back to his dinner in a dismissive gesture. The woman's face fell in disbelief. Tory didn't need to be near enough to hear the exchange. It was clear that the she had been shot down! The woman continued to look at him in disbelief as he continued eating his dinner, ignoring her. Finally she jumped up and stalked away, leaving behind a trail of curses.

Yikes...Tory would never act like that if she were shot down--not that it would ever happen since she never put herself out there like that. She couldn't stop smiling. It felt good knowing that while Tory didn't have a chance with the cutie, neither did miss Halle Berry!

Her order came and *sopa de couves* turned out to be stew that was filled with potato, collard greens, beef and red beans. There was a slight bite to it that she loved. Partnered with crusty bread and fresh squeezed lemonade and Tory was in culinary heaven.

The waitress returned to freshen her drink. "How is everything?"

"You were right. This is really good."

"I'll bring you the next dish."

Next? But the waitress whisked away in a flourish of colorful cloth, body thick but sensual.

She finished her soup and then a plate of clams was set before her. Mmmm, smothered in a garlic butter sauce. Slices of bread dipped into the sauce. Tory looked up at the waitress in appreciation.

"*Lapas.*" And her voice had a *ta da*, quality to it. "I hope you like clams."

"I love clams." The waitress smiled.

"I will bring your desert." Tory hadn't ordered desert in a year. But she would eat it, and then maybe curl up into a little ball of guilt later that night. Tory picked up the first clam and dug out the tender flesh. Perfectly cooked. As she ate, periodically she would peek up at the man from the bus. He was currently sipping coffee and seemed satisfied to sit quietly, showing no interest in the game on the big screen television or any of the other diners at the bar.

Tory fantasized at what she'd say if he turned around and saw her. Would he even remember her? She was still thinking these thoughts as she ate the pastry that the waitress set before her. When the meal was over Tory left a hefty tip. The waitress' eyes brightened. "Thank you so much!"

"No, thank you. That was an experience. So this is Portuguese food." It was more of a question then a statement.

"Well, actually Azores. There is a big difference. You should come back." She liked the waitress' accent.

"I will." Tory stood and gave the man at the bar one last look. He was sitting at the bar quietly and very still. Hmmm, if she weren't such a chicken she would go up and tell him hello. He looked like he could use someone to talk to. Instead she hurried out of the restaurant, glancing at her watch. It was dark and she was tired and her bus stop was several blocks away.

She walked to the bus stop as fast as she could; thinking that walking alone in an unfamiliar neighborhood especially at night was a pretty ill conceived idea. Next time, she'd be smart and call a cab.

She found her mind wandering back to the guy from the bus. Maybe he was Portuguese and this must be his neighborhood. That made perfect sense. It would be the bus stop prior to reaching hers. She wondered how often he ate here. Perhaps she would become very familiar with this place.

That night Tory drew a bath and soaked a week's worth of stress from her body. She put in her favorite oil from THE AFRICAN SPA and then after her bath she lotioned her skin until it felt like spun silk.

Tory felt as if there was very little about herself that she could be proud of, but she knew her complexion was perfect. How many times had she heard, 'You have such a pretty face?' It didn't take her long to realize that this was the only thing about herself that was pretty.

She brushed her shoulder length hair and then quickly rolled it. After brushing her teeth she sank into bed and fantasized about the man on the bus.

They Say Love is Blind

CHAPTER 2

When her alarm clock rang, Tory was prompt to get out of bed. She ate half a grapefruit and an egg white omelet. She then dressed in a pantsuit that accentuated her breasts but downplayed her 'everything else.'

Looking in her vanity mirror, she styled her hair then set it with hair spray, applied lipstick and a bit of eyeliner. She looked at her watch knowing that she had plenty of time to catch her 'regular bus'...and then chose to relax with a cup coffee instead.

Confidently, Tory slipped on charcoal pumps to match her suit and strolled down the street at a leisurely pace. She sat on the bench and actually waited for the bus to arrive. There would be no entertainment at her expense today!

When she stepped onto the bus, the first thing Tory did was to look for her favorite bus passenger and wasn't disappointed. He was in his usual seat.

She sat down next to him before paying her fare, pretending to search for change.

He turned slightly in his seat. "Good morning." His voice was deep with a pleasant low rumble. Her heart began to pound. He spoke first!

16

"Good morning. How are you today?" She said in a casual tone.

"I'm fine. May I put that money in for you?" He asked politely, holding out his hand for her change.

Her brow went up a notch. "Yes, thank you. I wouldn't want to fall on you again." She dropped the change into his hand her fingers brushing his palm slightly.

His full lips curved into a slow grin as he stood. "Totally my pleasure."

Tory's breath caught...that sounded like he was flirting...was he flirting with her? The man didn't even wait for the bus to slow or stop, he just stood and leaned, his muscles clear beneath his clothes, his ass worth two looks and Tory made sure that she looked twice.

When he sat back down, he reached between his feet to pat his duffel bag that was slid under the seat. He looked at her then. His eyes were golden brown and held her complete attention. They were heavily hooded bedroom eyes that made her want to swim in them...

"You didn't happen to eat at the Jewel of the Azores last night did you?"

Tory couldn't help but to gasp. "How did you know? I mean, I didn't think you saw me—I mean, I saw you at the bar."

He was nodding through all her flustered chatter. "Pardon me, I didn't introduce myself." He held out his hand and she placed hers within his, his thumb swept the back of her hand briefly and her nipples sprung to life.

"I'm Lee."

"I'm Victoria but most everyone calls me Tory."

He released her hand slowly. "Excuse me Tory, this is my stop." He reached above him and tugged the rope. She couldn't stop looking at the way his muscles flexed through the sleeves of his shirt. "On Wednesdays the restaurant has a dinner buffet. If you're adventurous you should come by."

Tory's heartbeat quickened with a jolt. It almost sounded like an invitation. Lee picked up his bag and gripped the pole as he stood.

"Maybe I'll see you." He called over his shoulder before disappearing out the door.

"Bye!" She called in return. Her eyes must have been as big as two saucers. She wanted to jump up and down and dance up the aisle! He had totally flirted!

The hoochie Mama sitting down from her was hating-on-her big time. Tory wanted to stand up and yell, *'that's right, bitch! He was flirting with me, not you!'* She settled for just smiling widely in the girl's direction. The hoochie Mama rolled her eyes.

After work Tory headed for the restaurant. It was Wednesday; buffet night. Lee had told her she should stop by. The obvious invitation was not lost on her!

When she finally made it to the restaurant she was limping painfully in the pumps that she had put on that morning. That was it! She had to leave a pair of running shoes in her drawer at work, or by the front door so that she could grab them as she hurried out. Her feet had swollen and she had been forced to sit down twice in the eight blocks since stepping off the bus, although not just because her feet were sore but because she was also just plain out of breath. She chastised herself for being so out of shape that she couldn't walk a few blocks without an oxygen mask.

The hostess recognized her from the night before. Like the waitress that she'd had on her last visit, the hostess was very pretty and carried her extra weight as if it wasn't something that she needed to lose. In fact, the plumpness of her body actually enhanced her beauty. But Tory quickly thought, I am not Portuguese or Azorean or some other exotic beauty. I am just fat.

"Hello, welcome back. Table for one?" She asked with a pleasant smile.

Tory cocked her head and strained to see the bar. "No...I think I'll just sit at the bar."

"Okay. Enjoy your meal."

19

"Thank you." She smoothed the wrinkles from her suit. Her feet stopped hurting when she saw Lee eating at the bar, smiling shyly she headed to him.

The waitress she'd had yesterday greeted her enthusiastically.

"Hi. Welcome back." She was carrying a pitcher of iced tea. Happily, Tory returned the greeting. The waitress reached the bar before her and refilled Lee's empty glass. She then slathered a passionate kiss on the top of his head.

Tory stopped. Her smile froze on her lips and then disappeared all together. Lee brought his arm up around her waist and gave her a quick squeeze, his arm lingering there as they joked quietly.

Tory turned and hurried out of the restaurant, passing the hostess who watched her with curious alarm. Her face was hot and probably flaming red through her light brown complexion. She had misread everything! Jesus, she had almost made a fool out of herself.

Tory hurried back down the street the way she had just come. When she reached the bus stop her eyes were red from the tears that she had angrily brushed away.

The next morning when the alarm went off, Tory thought fleetingly of calling in sick. She felt sick; her stomach was empty from skipping dinner the night before, but more than that her heart felt empty. So what if a man that she barely knew wasn't flirting with her? Only that it had made her so happy to think that he was and now that the feeling was gone, there was nothing else.

Big deal; except that it had made her think back to high school when she liked some stupid jock or some egotistical popular guy who wouldn't notice her in a million years. And that is why she had cried herself to sleep last night.

Dragging her pathetic self out of bed, Tory showered, then ate some toast and drank some juice in order to stop her stomach from complaining. Go to work, Tory, she said to herself. You have been late far too many times to just take off over some self-pity crap!

Moving into action she thought about the late bus and having to see Lee. She didn't want that! She didn't ever want to see him again. She would never be late for her first bus again!

Tory scowled as she watched her bus round the corner. Well that was it! She would get up an HOUR earlier each day. This was the last time that she'd catch the late bus. She plopped down on the bench, a scowl still on her face. When the bus arrived, she had her change in her hand ready. She placed it into the feeder and hurried past the incredibly, heart-breakingly gorgeous Lee, to a seat in the rear of the bus. She stared out the window, a new lump forming in her throat. He had not even looked at her.

"Excuse me, handsome." Tory snuck a peek to the front of the bus to see the hoochie mama, pole dancer that had mean-mugged her yesterday. She was, once again, apparently wearing her work clothes that consisted of a tight t-shirt, no bra and black skintight lycra pants. The woman sidled up next to Lee who looked ahead with no interest.

"Hey there? What's going on?" She asked, sticking her chest out at him.

Lee finally looked at her. "Not interested, sweetheart."

Half of the people on the bus started whooping in laughter. *Ha! That used to be directed at me.* Tory felt a smile tug at her lips. Miss hoochie stood up, mumbling curses under her breath and then she abruptly left the bus. A few moments later, Lee retrieved his duffel bag and followed suit. Whatever he was, you couldn't call him a ho, Tory thought. Dissed two gorgeous beauties in two days!

She stared out the window at him. For once, she was sitting on the side of the bus that allowed her to get a complete look at his body as he stepped off the bus; it would be the last time so she indulged herself and took a good look at him. He absently tossed his duffel bag over his shoulder and then dug into one of the many pockets. She saw him flick his wrist and for a split second thought that he had withdrawn a set of nunchucks. Then in alarm, she realized as the bus rushed past, exactly what he was holding; a white cane.

Tory craned her neck as the bus sped away. She caught a fleeting view of him heading purposefully down the street, the cane tapping periodically in front of him.

"Oh my God..." she gasped.

He's blind.

She sank into her seat. How? He had looked right at her yesterday with those gorgeous eyes. He did not look like a blind man! Wait a minute...How did he know that she had been in the Jewel of the Azores?

Tory felt hot and cold shivers travel up and down her body. Lee was blind.

CHAPTER 3

Tory was literally no good for the rest of the day. She made obvious filing mistakes, glaring typos and missed giving her phone customers complete answers to even their most mundane questions. If she was monitored today she would definitely earn-and deserve-a bad rating on her evaluation.

After work that evening, her feet would not allow her to step off the bus at her normal stop. She sat there and continued the ride until she reached the familiar last stop before The Jewel of the Azores restaurant. She must be getting used to the long walk because the burning ache in her calves and shins did not return. She finally reached the restaurant, out of breath but not in pain. When the hostess saw her, she gave Tory a doubtful look before smiling carefully at her.

Tory gestured to the bar. "I'm just going to have a seat at the bar." Tory spoke apologetically. She headed there, purposefully. But as she saw Lee eating, her resolve began to weaken. With one last shuddering breath, she pushed on until she was standing at the empty seat next to him.

"Hello," Tory said.

He looked at her. "Tory, hi." He smiled in a soft, sexy way. "Have a seat and join me for dinner." She couldn't help but to examine his eyes. They were looking right at her...

"Okay." She took the stool next to him, peeking at his bowl of half finished stew. "Looks like *sopa de couve,*" she said absently.

He almost choked in surprise then smiled at her happily. "You said that perfectly. *De certeza que não tens uma costela Portuguesa?"*

She blushed. "I don't speak Portuguese other then *sopa de couves.*"

He chuckled. "I asked if you are sure that you don't have a Portuguese rib." She could hear a slight accent when he spoke. It was very sexy. "I missed you at the buffet yesterday." He suddenly had a serious look on his face. "Maybe next time, eh?"

Tory's eyes were big when the same waitress that had served her, as well as lavished Lee with a huge kiss, approached with a place setting and a menu. She had a huge smile on her face, which she directed to Tory.

"Hello again. Leandro you better be on your best behavior. This is a nice lady." The waitress busily placed the silverware on the bar while Lee held up his hands innocently.

"I'm nice too. Stop trying to scare her away." He was joking but his words caused Torys heartbeat to quicken.

"Tory, this is my sister, Macey. And Macey, this is Victoria; Tory."

"Sister?" Her mouth was hanging opened. If Macey noticed that she was acting oddly, she hid it well, asking if she wanted lemonade to which she just nodded silently. Macey hurried away with a slight bounce to her rounded posterior.

When they were alone again Lee stared at her intently. "I have four sisters. Two of them own this restaurant and the other's work for them. I eat here almost every day." He smiled. "I grew up on this cooking, so I guess I'm addicted to it, I'm not sure if that's an endorsement or not."

Sister. She wanted to kick herself. Lee's sister returned with fresh lemonade for her and an iced tea for him.

"Do you know what you want?" She asked Tory who was trying to understand the question, her mind still addled at her huge mistake.

"Oh!" She hadn't even looked at the menu.

"Shall I recommend something?" Lee offered. She nodded and then remembered that he couldn't see.

"Yes."

"What are your thoughts on beans?" he asked. Her brow went up slightly.

"They taste good."

He chuckled and then she did as well. "*Feijoada*," he directed to his sister. "And your thoughts on pork? Traditionally this dish is served with pork but it can be changed out with *chouriço,* which is sausage."

"I like both."

"Both, then, Macey." Oops! She didn't mean she wanted both. He must think she is a glutton. When his sister retreated with her order Tory turned to him curiously.

"What am I about to eat?"

"Nothing too adventurous. Just beans and rice with some vegetables and meat." As she looked at him sitting so comfortable and friendly she couldn't believe how stupid she'd been. He reached for his glass of iced tea and she noted that his hand moved slowly so that he wouldn't knock it over.

"Can I ask you a question?" He spoke after taking a liberal drink.

Uh oh. "Is this going to be embarrassing?"

"Yes." The corners of his mouth lifted into a smile.

"Okay, shoot." She said shyly.

"Why do you run for the bus every day?"

She gave him a shocked smile. "What do you mean, *everyday*?! I didn't run Wednesday!"

Lee nodded, hiding his look of amusement. "You didn't run today, either." Ah, so he knew that she had been on the bus. Tory wanted to bury her head in the ground. He continued, "Which brings me to my next question: Did you sic that crazy woman from the bus on me?"

Suddenly she was laughing hard and trying not to be the center of attention in the restaurant. Still, she almost lost her seat on the barstool. "Oh my God, that was so funny! I swear, I thought she was going to smack you!"

"I was hoping that I'd never have the privilege of speaking to that one."

"You say that as if it's a curse to have beautiful women approach you."

"No, Tory." He said seriously. "I just know what I like and I'm not settling for anything less." He stared at her so hard that her eyes were the ones to drop. Damn, a blind man had just stared her down.

Macey returned with a huge platter of food. White rice was to one side and the rest was filled with beans that looked as if it had been stewed with vegetables and hunks of meat. Her stomach growled long and loud, leaving her mortified.

She peeked at Lee who was eating the last of his soup as if he hadn't heard. She slowly ate a spoonful of some of the beans. "Mmm." She murmured in appreciation.

"So I did good in choosing for you?"

"Very good." Rice, beans, vegetables and meat; how could it get better than that? She glanced at him. She just had to know, and since he had begun by asking her a question she felt that the door was open.

"Can I ask you a question?"

"Of course." He pushed back his bowl and gave her his full attention.

"How did you see me when I was here the other day?" She was blushing furiously that he might think that she was bringing up a sensitive subject. Instead he gave her an easy smile. It made her heart flutter and the adrenalin rush to her head.

"I heard you."

"Was I that loud?"

"I recognized the sound of your voice. And no. You weren't talking very loud. I can just hear very well."

"You're...totally blind?"

"Yes." He watched her intently. "I used to be able to see some...hazy, though, and shadowy. But that's been a long time ago." He seemed absolutely relaxed as he talked about this thing that must be incredibly devastating. She cleared her throat, and pushed on.

"It really seems like you're looking at me right now."

"Ahh." He turned away from her and reached for his iced tea.

"I mean, I'm not complaining! It's just that...I thought you were looking at me."

Lee smiled and looked at her again, looked her right in the eyes. "I am looking at you, Tory. I can't see you with my eyes, but I can look at you just fine." He straightened in his stool. "I know exactly where you are by your voice. I know exactly where to look." She considered his words as she ate. He really couldn't see her. She took a big spoonful of food and chewed it quickly, so that she could continue talking without shooting food out of her mouth at him.

"So...are you married, have a boyfriend?" He asked.

She shook her head quickly, almost choking. "No." Her face was turning red again. "I'm single."

"Just for the record, so am I."

She stared at him with big eyes. Flirting again? Was this flirting, or was this just making friendly conversation? God, why couldn't she tell the difference?! She was doubting herself now. In a moment of desperation she just blurted out. "Ok, I'm going to be honest here. I'm not too swift in this area, but are you flirting with me?"

Any look of amusement fell from his face. He watched her with a very serious expression. "Tory,

I like you. I'll just make it plain, ok? I'd like to get to know you."

Tory was quiet as she digested his words, trying to find a hidden meaning. After she examined it from all angles she found that there was nothing lurking behind those words. He liked her. Her heart was beating a mile a minute and breathing was becoming a real chore. Lee said that he liked her...but now the big question.

"Why?"

That question seemed to throw him for a loop because he opened and then closed his mouth, finally turning back to his soup as if to contemplate the last remnants that remained in the bottom of his bow.

Maybe she would kick herself for this later, but the answer to that one simple question was the most important thing in the world to Tory right now.

"What made you even notice me? I'm sorry if I'm putting you on the spot-"

"It's not that." He turned to face her again. "It's just that I'm not usually this forward. I mean, I don't know anything about you yet...and the answer to that question might offend you."

Offend her? She didn't know if she should prompt him to continue, or not. But she remained silent. His hands clasped in his lap and he sighed deeply.

"I noticed you because you run for the bus every day."

"What?" She looked at him in confusion.

He sighed. "You run for the bus every day and when you get on you sound like you've just made love...and have been thoroughly satisfied." Tory's heart jumped in her chest, her cheeks flamed. He continued. "The first time I heard that...I could barely stand up to get off the bus. I look forward to that sound every day, Tory. And then, one day you fell into my lap and...well, I wasn't lying when I said that it was truly my pleasure."

Tory's mouth gaped open and she was momentarily speechless. No man had ever said anything so sexy to her in her entire life! She was practically trembling with emotion—and another, more earthy, sensual feeling that sprouted from her stomach and spread warm fingers between her thighs and across her puckering nipples.

She finally blew out a slow calming breath and looked at Lee who was still awaiting her reaction. Swiftly she leaned over to kiss his cheek.

He turned to her, surprised, his mouth slightly ajar, lips full and delicious; so much so that Tory could barely take her eyes from them.

"You are very sweet." He said honestly. "Can I see you?"

She searched his face before answering. "Yes."

Lee reached out tentatively. His fingertips came in contact with her cheeks first. Lightly he traced its contours. His eyes took on a distant expression as he concentrated. His fingertips moved lightly to her ears and then down her neck and up the back, over her hairline which was pulled up into a French twist. Quickly he rubbed a few strands of her hair through his fingertips.

It wasn't fine like his hair or his sister's hair. Did he even know that she was African American? Did that matter to him?

His fingers moved to her forehead and then ever-so-lightly over her eyes, nose, than lips. At her lips he hesitated and then using one thumb, dragged her bottom lip down slightly.

Before thinking, she lightly drew her lips together and kissed the tip of his finger, then she flushed, embarrassed. What was she doing?!

Lee tilted his head, perhaps thinking the same thing. But then his fingers traveled across her shoulders, boldly grazed over her breasts — which caused her breathing to become heavier. His hands, still travelling downward moved over her belly and then lightly up her sides.

By that time, Tory could barely catch her breath. She didn't want him to hear her breathing heavy because she knew that's how he 'saw' her, with his ears and now with his hands. But wishing something didn't prevent it from happening and her nipples ached to be touched, the space between her legs thrummed almost painfully.

"Thank you." He whispered while allowing his hands to drop from her body.

"I...better-" She stood, "it's getting late." She picked up her purse with shaky hands and began digging into it for money. "How much is this-?" She was incredibly uncomfortable.

"Tory, it's on me. Please. Let me walk you to your car or call you a cab."

She shook her head. "No. I can just take the bus."

"Are you sure?" A look of disappointment crossed his face.

She nodded. When he didn't respond she quickly said yes.

"Well let me at least walk you to the bus stop-"

"You don't have to do that."

He suddenly looked unhappy. His expression fell and a shadow replaced the disappointment. She suddenly realized that it appeared as if she was giving him the brush off, or that she didn't think that he was capable of escorting her. In actuality, it was something much more basic; Tory was so turned-on that she thought a strong wind might send her over the edge! She just wanted to get away from the source of her torment as quickly as she could.

"Actually...it is pretty dark. Would you walk with me?" He nodded and reached into his pocket for his wallet, pulling out several bills, which he dropped onto the bar.

"You can be my cane tonight." He held out his arm for her.

His cane! She hoped she wouldn't cause him to trip. She slipped her fingers around his arm, unable to stop herself from brushing his biceps with the back of her fingers. Hmmm, hard as a rock.

"Just walk at a normal pace." Tory headed to the entrance. The hostess gave her an appraising look before telling them good night.

"Is that one of your sisters?"

"No. That's Rosalind. I grew up with her, though." Tory wasn't very swift with certain things, but she could easily see when a woman felt that she had a stake in a man, and Rosalind had that look. Tory paused and slowly stepped across the threshold. He crossed smoothly a moment after her.

"I'm sorry about making you uncomfortable in there." She was about to deny it but he continued. "We discussed some things that I definitely would not have touched with a ten foot pole until...I knew you a lot better." He glanced at her and innocently licked his lips, causing a strange effect in the pit of her stomach; it felt like someone had touched her with a tazer! He wanted to know her better…

"It's ok." She responded too quickly. "It's just that all this time I thought I sounded like a fat lady breathing heavy." He didn't respond and she covered the uncomfortable silence. "I don't remember seeing you on that bus before. I don't ride it every day..." but she would have remembered him.

"I moved here from across town. I used to come this way to eat at the Jewel a few times a week and to visit my sisters. I think I just decided to sacrifice proximity to work for proximity to family. It was a smart move."

"What do you do?"

"I work for a publishing company converting books to Braille. We work with a lot of instructional manuals, and teaching aids, but also on demand. If someone wants the latest Stephen King novel then we will convert it for them."

"Do you like doing that type of work?"

"I love it. I can set my own hours, work from home when I want. All I need is to meet my deadlines. Plus I get to learn new things. I converted an instructional manual for how to build a kit car. I don't know too many visually impaired car builders but…hey."

Tory chuckled. Lee had a sense of humor and he didn't seem to view his blindness as an untouchable topic. They came to the curb marking the end of the block and Tory abruptly stopped walking. "Okay, in about three steps from here we're going to come to the curb."

Lee's lip curled in amusement.

"Thank you, Tory. Just take the step first and I'll follow." She did and smoothly he followed. She gave him an impressed look.

"What?" He asked, turning to her.

She was speechless. Sometimes like this, it was like he could really see her. "How did you know that I was looking at you?"

Once she had guided him back to the next curb and stepped onto the walk, he stopped and turned to her. "Close your eyes." She did, after a slight hesitation. "Are they closed?"

"Yes." He didn't speak. She concentrated on the darkness. Then she felt something move past her face and her head flinched back a fraction of an inch.

"Did you feel that?"

Tory opened her eyes, "Yeah. What did you do?"

"What did it feel like I did?"

She thought for a moment. "You waved your hand in front of my face."

"*Munte bom!*" He said. "Very good. That's exactly what I did."

"Moon-te..." She tried to repeat.

"*Munte.*" He corrected her pronunciation. "Moo-in-two *bom*. Very good."

"*Munte bom,*" she said.

"Very good, *bela.*"

"*Bela*?"

"Beautiful."

She grinned shyly.

"It's the first thing a person wants to do when they find out you're blind," he continued. "So, to answer your question...if you could sense that after being blind for five seconds imagine how much I can sense after being blind all of my life."

"Wow." He took her arm and gently wrapped it around his and they continued walking.

"Tory?"

"Yes?"

"Why do you run for the bus every day?"

She laughed. He was not letting that go. "Because...I'm a procrastinator. Okay? Time seems to slip by me despite my good intentions. Besides," she continued shyly. "If you didn't hear me breathing heavy in the morning you'd have to rely on the hoochie Mama from the bus to titillate you."

He chuckled. "Or I can just wait for the bus driver to take off real fast and cause you to fall into my lap again."

Tory squeezed his arm in good humor and he sighed. "Tell me about yourself; everything. I want to feel like I know you--more than I already do."

As they walked the remaining eight blocks, arm in arm, Tory explained about being an only child. She thought he was so lucky to have such a big family. She hadn't really been anywhere exciting, not much further then the same city where she had been born and raised. Her job was pretty boring which made it tedious. She spent all day on the telephone doing customer service and filling orders for a major department store. And her love life...well she didn't even bring that up.

Lee was the one to stop when they got to the bus stop; Tory had been so preoccupied answering his questions that she had forgotten all about leading him and it seemed that it was he that was now leading her.

"Tory, I can't believe that you've never been further than Kentucky!" He led her to the bench and they sat down. She winced. Her feet ached and her body was tight.

"Not having a car has made that difficult." He just raised a brow.

"When will your bus arrive?" She dug into her bag for the bus schedule. "Less than ten minutes." He reached for her hand. "Tired?"

She smiled shyly. "Yes. This is quite a walk for me." She looked at her hand in his; hers brown and his much paler.

"You were limping near the end. Maybe next time we can meet...some place closer?"

"Oh." She tried to stay very cool but her heart was beating a mile a minute. "Like, where?"

"Well, I don't go out all that much. But I do like live music. Club Kat is right across the street..." She glanced where he gestured. She could hear a live band playing. It wasn't what she would normally listen to but the beat was hard and it made her want to move her body. She turned to him in time to see an expectant, hopeful look on his face. Was that a look of insecurity? How is it that a man as sexy as him could ever be insecure? She gripped his hand.

"That sounds like fun, Lee."

He seemed to relax. "Tomorrow is Friday; how is that?"

"Can I ask you a question first?"

"Certainly."

"What's your full name?"

He gave her a twisted smile. "I'm so sorry. I've asked you out for a date and you know nothing about me." The bus rounded the corner and Tory's smile dropped. "Let me introduce myself before that bus whisks you away. I'm Leandro Eduardo das Torres...or just Lee Torres." He frowned and cocked his head, standing with her hand still clasped in his. So, give me your phone number and I'll call you later tonight."

"Just call it out to you?"

40

"Yes." He smiled. "I have a great memory." She did as he asked and watched him repeat it once before nodding his head. The bus pulled up in front of them and she reluctantly slipped her hand from his grip.

"Bye, *bela*."

Her body tingled at that word. "Bye, Lee." She climbed onto the bus and watched him until the bus rounded the block. A date. Oh God, a date with the sexy man from the bus; Leandro Eduardo das Torres! She closed her eyes, collapsing back against the seat.

Tory got home and didn't know what to do with herself. He said he'd call tonight. She changed out of her work clothes—especially the shoes, putting on her furry slippers. Then she sat curled up in her armchair with her cell phone right at her fingertips. She replayed her entire evening with him, blushing when she said something foolish, tingling when he did something sexy.

"*Bela*..." She said quietly and then the phone rang. She jumped, sending it falling to the floor. "Oh no!" She leaped up and went scampering for it, hoping that it hadn't shattered! It rang again and a relieved gust issued from her lungs.

"Hello?" She said, trying to sound calm.

"*Ola*, Tory."

It was him! "*Ola*, Lee."

"Were you busy?"

"No." She started pacing nervously. "I was just relaxing." She sat down quickly and pretended to relax.

"Thank you for coming out. I enjoyed spending time with you."

"Thanks for inviting me." She said shyly.

"Tomorrow, meet me at the club. I'll be outside waiting for you. Is that okay?"

"Okay. That sounds great."

"Did you want to meet right after work...or did you want to go home first...?"

"Umm. How about right after work? Then there's no chance of me missing the bus and leaving you waiting." He chuckled.

"Sounds like a plan."

"Then I should see you a few minutes after six."

"Okay. *Adeus*, Tory."

"*Adeus*, Lee." She hung up the phone and shook her head, a smile still on her face. She could not believe how things had worked out.

CHAPTER 4

The next day, Tory intentionally missed her normal bus. She wore a dress that complimented her curves and slipped on comfortable heels. Even though her feet protested due to all of the walking she'd done this week, she figured it would okay since her bus stop wasn't far from any of her destinations. Besides, bigger girls looked great in heels; especially if they knew how to do a model walk, and she'd practiced perfecting that long ago.

When she saw the bus rounding the corner, she stood up from her seat on the bench, her heart pitter-pattering in anticipation of seeing Lee again. Her cheeks grew warm as she remembered the fantasies that she'd had about him the night before. He was sitting in his regular seat and Tory hurried to grip the pole since she'd figured out the bus driver's game.

"Hi, Lee." She said shyly.

"Good morning." He smiled. "Let me put your money in and you can sit down here by me." His hand was held out and she dropped the coins into his waiting palm. His movement was sensual and slow as he rose from his seat, absently clutching the pole as he slipped her coins into the feeder. In the process he managed to brush her backside as she stepped around him in order to sit down.

She perched herself into the empty seat next to his and when he sat down, his hand reached out and lightly brushed her shoulder, than he sat down and looked at her. "You weren't limping today. Do your feet feel better?"

"Much."

"Good, I don't want to be forced to remove your shoes and give you a good rub down tonight." Every muscle in Tory's lower body tightened. She watched Lee's playful expression. He was such a flirt! Did he even know how much his words affected her? By the look on his face, he did.

"That would be my pleasure." She said seriously, giving him back his own line.

He suddenly chuckled. "I'm looking forward to tonight."

She smiled, enjoying the game of seduction and double entendre. "Me, too, Lee." She was suddenly serious. "It was all I could think about last night..."

He licked his full lips and she had to force herself to remember that she didn't need to be at work fully turned on with no outlet! Lee tilted his head slightly.

"I think that we're going to have fun tonight. I did some research on the net and found that the band that's playing tonight is Reggaeton and they have a lot of Ska influences."

"Reggae...Tone? I know Reggae, but never heard of Reggaeton."

"Really? Wow, girl, I'm going to have to show you something." He said with pleasure. "Reggaeton is

like...dancehall music. It would be more like a hip hop reggae. You've heard of Shaba Ranks, right?"

"Yeah." She nodded.

"That's Reggaeton. Mix Beenie man with Lil Wayne."

"Ooo, that's going to be nice."

He licked his lips again and then grabbed his duffel bag and stood. "This is my stop. I hope you're up for some dancing tonight, because I can dance all night long!" He was halfway down the stairs before he called over his shoulder. "See you tonight, Bela."

"Bye Lee!" Her brow was raised doubtfully...dance all night? Damn! Maybe she could take a pain pill since her feet were already sore. Still, the idea of dancing the night away with a sexy Latin guy was appealing despite the corns developing on her feet!

Work went super slow. At lunch she tried to select something to eat that wouldn't talk to her later during her date, which meant no onions, fish, or bean burrito. She settled on a ham sandwich and a cup of chicken noodle soup just to make sure that her stomach wouldn't be doing any embarrassing growling.

When Tory finally stepped off the bus across the street from Club Kat, her eyes immediately searched for Lee and there he stood near the entrance. No cane in sight, he stood patiently waiting for her arrival. It sent a thrill through her-- that, as well as the fact that he looked really sexy. He was wearing black slacks, a casual t-shirt and a black jacket. She hurried across the street and when she was just a few feet from him, he smiled broadly and greeted her first.

"Tory. Hello."

"And how did you know it was me before I even said hi?"

He offered her his arm. "Remember, that I can see pretty well with my other senses. Are you ready for some Reggaeton? It's taking all of my will power not to stand out here and dance...but then people would throw me money."

She put her arm through his. "They wouldn't even know that you can't see."

"No. You can be my cane again. And I got our tickets online when I checked the itinerary."

"You use the computer?" He mentioned that earlier but she hadn't had time to ask him about it.

"Yes, all of the time. Actually, the computer is essential for my job." She led him into the entrance of the club and through a small crowding of people as he spoke. "I use a system called JAWS that reads the material for me. But most computers have an automatic text to voice program built in."

"Ohhh, gotcha."

"I have a little British woman that reads to me on a daily basis," he joked.

"Your computer has a British accent?"

"Or any accent I want it to have."

"Did you name her? I bet you have a name for her."

He chuckled. "I do actually. Her name is Nancy. Nancy has quite the sexy voice when she's reading a Dr. Suess book for me to transcribe." Tory couldn't help but to laugh. Lee had a great sense of humor. He looked at her. "Of course, it's not as sexy as that laugh of yours."

She blushed and didn't know what to say. "Thank you," she finally replied.

"*De nada.*" They reached a window with a coat check and a girl with a blue Mohawk and five facial piercings greeted them.

"Welcome to Club Kat. For two?"

"Yes. I paid online." Lee responded. He gave his name and she slid two tickets to them. Tory retrieved them and then led them down a short flight of stairs. The music was already loud before they had even entered the room and the beat was thumping! She liked it already.

The club was popular, that was evident. Even at barely six thirty there were a lot of people on the dance floor. It was a mix of all kinds of people; black, Latin, whites and there was no specific age. She saw younger college age men and woman just as she saw more mature couples. The one constant is that they loved moving their bodies wildly to the Reggaeton beat. She led him to a small round table that wouldn't be large enough to hold her elbow.

He sat down and briefly placed his hands on both sides of the round table before leaning towards her and speaking over the loud music. "Do you want a drink?"

She didn't drink much since she didn't do much socializing and drinking alone was no fun.

"A wine cooler would be nice."

"Do you like sweet wine?"

"Yeah. I guess I'm not a wine connoisseur or anything. But I would like something sweet and fruity." He nodded. "Is there a waitress or just a bartender?"

"Both." She looked around and waved a waitress over. "One is heading our way now."

"I'm going to order you something good. Trust me." The waitress was young and cute wearing an extra short tube skirt and a tan that could not be natural.

"Would you like to order drinks? Tapas are complimentary with a drink order." She had an accent...not quite like Lee who only had an accent when speaking Portuguese, and Tory could sense a different dialect.

"Sangria for the lady and *cerveja* for me."

"*Cerveja? Você é Português?*"

"Portuguese, yes."

"Ahh." She gave him a lingering look and Tory crossed her feet under the table in annoyance. No this woman was not flirting with her date right in front of her?! The waitress smiled at Lee. "Any particular brand of beer?"

"Do you have Super Bock?"

"But of course." She paused and when no one responded she spoke in a rush. "I'll be right back with your drinks and two complimentary tapas." Tory hid a smirk. Lee would not be giving that one any secret looks.

"Do you care if I move my chair next to yours? I feel like I'm on the other side of the world."

49

"The other side of the world with this little table? Our knees are practically touching."

He moved his leg back and forth against her knee. "I know. But more of us can touch if I'm sitting next to you."

Again she was at a loss for words. "That would be nice." He brought his chair around so that they both were facing the dancers and stage where the band would later appear. When he was settled he put his arm around the back of her chair and spoke next to her ear. "This is better. Now I can talk to you without screaming."

Chills traveled up her body as the slight puffs of air from his mouth touched her skin, and not to mention the way the sound of his low voice reverberated through her body. She nodded, knowing that he was close enough that he would feel even her slightest tremble. Feeling adventurous, she suddenly turned and placed her lips next to his ear to whisper.

"This is much nicer than sitting across from each other. Good idea." She enjoyed feeling his hard body right next to hers. His arm draped over her chair allowed his hand to rest lightly against her shoulder and she decided that she loved touching and being touched by him.

Lee's body was moving to the beat of the music. She could tell that he longed to be out on the floor dancing. Her body began to sway unconsciously along with his.

He put his hand on her arm and leaned in to whisper to her again. "I am going to teach you how to dance the way we do back home."

"Oh...kay." Was her nervous response.

"Don't be afraid. Trust me."

The waitress returned then when they were whispering to each other. She slid two plates onto the table.

"I trust you." Tory whispered back.

"Good, because I want you to have fun."

"Um..." The waitress spoke. "It's happy hour. Your beer is on the international menu so it doesn't normally count for one dollar but I can hook you up." She winked at him. He was smiling as he turned his gaze to the waitress.

"Thank you. One dollar beer and free tapas? Great deal, isn't it, *bela*?"

"It is." She snuggled against him and smirked at the waitress. "We'll definitely have to come back.

"The waitress gave her a confused look. It said, 'here I am with my tiny waistline and I'm available'...well that's what Tory read into her look.

"Sorry," the waitress spoke in a clipped tone. "Your drink wasn't on special. That will be six dollars please."

Lee reached into his pocket and pulled out his wallet. He thumbed through several bills and when he reached the last; a ten, he gave it to her. "Can you bring us two glasses of ice water? We're about to work up a big sweat. And keep the change please." She took the money and left.

"Mmm, smells good. What is it?" He asked.

"Um...mine is a plate of potato chips. Yours is wontons and a dipping sauce."

Lee reached for one of her chips and placed it in his mouth. His brow went up. "No, not just potato chips; HOMEMADE potato chips. This place is known for their handmade chips deep fried in duck butter and there should be a shaving of white truffles over it."

She gave him an openmouthed look. "Computer research, or are you just that good?"

He chuckled. "I research pretty much everything. Try it. It's good."

She put a potato chip in her mouth. "Mmm." She chewed, savoring the taste. It was warm from the fryer, crispy yet moist and the duck oil added a hint of flavor that was hard to place. And white truffles? "This is free?"

"Yep." He said after chewing another chip. "The white truffle adds a hint of salt."

"Is that the white truffle? I wasn't sure. Wow, that's good."

He drank some of his beer and she picked up her glass of sangria and took a short drink. Then she took a longer one.

He gave her a steady, expectant look. "Do you like it?"

"It's good. Not too strong, and fruity...just what I wanted." He nodded.

"Shall we try the wontons...um, when I did the research I read that these are probably deep fried mushroom ravioli and the sauce is a mayonnaise aioli."

She chuckled. "That sounds a lot more appetizing then potato chips and wontons." The waitress returned with their ice water. She placed it on the table and disappeared without a word. They drank, and munched and just when her cheeks began to feel flushed from the liquor and her feet kept tapping to the rhythm of the music, Lee stood and took of his jacket, placing it neatly behind his chair.

She was so busy looking at the outline of his muscles through the shortsleeved shirt and the definition of his chest muscles that she didn't immediately notice that his hand was held out to her.

"May I have this dance?"

She sputtered, expecting this but still not prepared to shake her 'stuff' on the dance floor with people watching. "Guys usually say that when there is something slow playing..." The current song had a funky, hiphop beat and the band members were chanting something in a foreign language. The crowd had picked up the chorus and was chanting along. She placed her hand in his and came to her feet.

"What are they saying?" She asked as she led them to the dance floor.

"I...uh...better not say."

"Oh my goodness." She stopped when she found a place where she hoped they wouldn't get trampled. "Watch me." He brought his arms up, clapped his hands repeatedly and began gyrating to the beat...just like everyone else. His hips moved seductively, yet to the tempo of the music. Then he slowed his movements down a bit and reached out for her. She placed her hand in his and he put his other hand on her hips.

"Do what I do!" He yelled above the music.

She watched the way his feet moved, shuffling and stomping and mimicked it. Once she stopped, worrying about how she looked, but before too long she felt the music guide her movements and then the steps became more natural.

His hands on her hips monitored her movements and he smiled. "That's it! You're doing great, Tory!"

"She laughed. The sangria, the music and the closeness of Lee's body made everything feel dreamlike. Watching him move so confidently and effortlessly loosened her up, allowing her to express herself in a way that she'd never felt comfortable doing before—not even in the privacy of her home.

They danced and as the music moved from one song to another, so did his movements. He pulled her gently into his arms and she discovered that two people could also dance to a fast song in perfect synch. He slowed his movements and made them simple and repetitious until she was dancing in his arms.

"I'm going to spin you."

"Not in these heels!"

"To late..." He spun her and when she stumbled he saved her easily with his strong arms around her waist. "When I'm done with you Tory, you will be doing three spins effortlessly."

"Not tonight, I won't...unless you want me to get sick on you."

All amusement left his face. "Oh, I don't intend to be done with you in just one night."

Instead of being shy and embarrassed, Tory slid her hand up to his shoulders. "I'm glad. I think I'd like to learn to spin three times."

"I can teach you that, and more. Like how to dip. Shall I?"

"Ok."

He suddenly clutched her to him. One hand stayed around her waist, the other slid down the side of her body, over her rear end, down her thigh. He tilted her backward just as his hand on her leg lifted it enough that her inner knee now straddled his thigh.

She gasped and put her arms around his neck, clinging to him before she went crashing to the floor.

"I got you. You're not going to fall." He held her firmly in his grip for a few moments before he righted her. Tory's breath came in excited gusts. His hard body had been flush against hers...and he felt so good. She had never wanted to kiss someone so badly in all of her life. When his face had been inches from hers and his hooded eyes were on her; his attention on her and no one else...she had felt that they were the only two people in the world.

"Getting tired?" He asked.

"Can we sit down for a while? I can use some of that water."

"Let's go to the bar and get fresh drinks. I don't want anyone slipping you a roofie." She wondered who would want to slip her a roofie with all of these gorgeous women in the room...half of which was looking at her man. If anyone needed to be careful of a roofie it was him!

They got their water and sat down at their table. Their plates had been whisked away leaving them room for their bottled water. He put his arm around her again and unconsciously she leaned into his body.

"I hope I didn't tire you out too much."

"No. I've been missing my workouts, so I needed it." He didn't comment and after a lengthy pause she decided to ask him a question that she'd been curious about.

"Lee, what is Azores?"

He seemed happy about the question. His thumb stroked her shoulder lightly, where it touched his arm as it rested along the back of her chair.

"Do you know what an archipelago is?"

"Uhm...no."

He smiled. "It's basically a cluster of islands. The Azores is a Portuguese archipelago made up of volcanic islands in the North Atlantic Ocean. I grew up on the Flores Island. There are others; nine major ones in all. I grew up on Flores; named this because of the many beautiful flowers."

"That sounds beautiful."

"It's small and it is beautiful. There are not even five thousand people on the entire island. And because the Islands are volcanic, there are hot springs."

"Oh you can bathe in them!"

"There are some very nice bathing spots called *termas*. But there are also some springs that are so hot that they are only used for cooking; *furnas*. My family would travel to the spring in the morning and put a pot of stew in the earth and six hours later there was lunch. Azoreans are very proud

Portuguese, just as there are proud Brazilian Portuguese. But we see ourselves as very uniquely different. We're as proud of our culture as we are of our islands. We have some of the tallest mountains in the entire world, which means we also have some of the best waterfalls. Everything is either volcanic rock or lush green."

He spoke with so much pride that Tory found herself smiling.

"So why did you leave such a beautiful place?"

"My parents moved us to the States so that they could make money. But once we were here, me and my brothers and sisters integrated into the American culture while my parents later returned to the island to retire. We have a saying in the Azores. *Vou morrer pra minha terra;* I will die in my homeland. My parents live by that saying."

She gave him a steady look. "You miss it don't you?"

He nodded. "Being blind on an island is great. I can run, sprint even. And the only thing to run into is...the end of the Island." He had a wistful look on his face. "In my village everyone knew me and I knew them. People would yell out, 'watch out for that! Don't knock that over! You're going to step on that!' Even though there are a lot of tourists and Island living is very modern now, there is still a very quaint quality about it." She found herself wishing that she could see this beautiful paradise.

"Lee, what caused your blindness?" She had been curious about this since she had discovered his blindness but didn't know how to ask. But he seemed so open and secure with himself that she hoped he wouldn't mind her probing.

"Actually I was born sighted. My mother went into labor too early and I was premature. I was in an incubator for several weeks. The harsh lights is what caused my loss of sight."

"Oh God, that's horrible." Her hand unconsciously stroked his and she felt him shiver at the contact. "Is there anything that can be done to correct it?"

He placed his hand over hers, gently moving his thumb over her knuckles. "No, but it doesn't bother me. I don't know anything different. My family is very big; four sisters and three brothers and no room for special treatment. I fell, and got bumped and bruised until I figured out how not to fall and get bumps and bruises." He had a slight smile as he remembered the things he described. "When I was young I thought sight was...imagination. Like watching television; I thought that everyone listened to it just the way that they listened to the radio. The descriptions my family gave me were just...interpretation.

"For me vision is physical; getting hugs by my mother, wrestling with my brothers, playing with my sisters, hanging out in the field with the other kids—It's not the same as it is for the rest of the world. I'm not the same. My likes and dislikes are based on my comfort zone. I don't like spare ribs because they're messy, or Chinese food because I don't know what's in it." She grinned at that. "But I like hugs from my Mom because her arms around me feels like a safety net. I could put my head anywhere on her body and fall asleep feeling safe and in complete comfort.

"Not being able to see with my eyes allowed me to see differently, but just as accurately. My father's bones pop when he moves and I know whenever he's around and that everything is going to be alright. My brothers have always had my back. Carlo has asthma and I know when we've been playing too hard and he has to rest. Francie would let me sit on the seat of her ten speed whenever she had to run an errand into town for my Mom. And I'd throw my head back and let the breeze hit my face. Macey always chewed bubble gum and popped it loud so I knew to look for the smell of sweet gum whenever I needed to find her." He chuckled. Tory was totally mesmerized by his words.

"I like raindrops—it sounds alive. I like to touch and feel what's around me. I love cold on my tongue. It's more than a sensation to me; I assign it an emotion; it's like...a feeling of hope." He paused. "But what holds no appeal to me, Tory, is skinny women..." His hooded eyes were intent on her face. "...with their sharp bones poking into me. Feeling someone's rib bones through their skin doesn't interest me in the least. Teeny perky breast might be alright for some. Breasts that I can hold and bury my face into is much more appealing. When legs wrap around my body, I want to be gripping thighs and ass.

"Tory, your skin, your body, is soft and full and alive. You are full and buxom and that's what turns me on. This..." His hand slid down her waist "...is my comfort zone."

She was completely blown away by his words. He wasn't just a gorgeous man that could see beyond her weight. He was a gorgeous man that found her desirable because of it.

"To hear a guy like you...say something like that...it's just so hard to believe." She said shyly. "You're just too good to be true."

"Not everybody would think that. Tory. I'm a blind man to most women. Maybe not in the beginning. But in the end, that's all I am." He leaned forward and gave her a slight kiss on the lips. "But thank you for saying that I'm too good to be true, and believing it."

Her eyes were now hooded as she contemplated the feel of his lips on hers. "Would you...do that again?" She said in a husky whisper.

He smiled, lips only an inch from hers. "Gladly." Lee raised his hand to her face. Gentle fingers stroked her cheek as he leaned forward with parted lips. Tory's breath felt paralyzed in her chest. She couldn't breathe, she couldn't think. All she could do was to react. Her hand came up to hold his head in place, her fingers burying themselves in his golden brown hair.

A soft groan issued from his throat and his own hand moved upward to hold her head gently as his tongue traced over her lips, exploring the depths of her mouth with feather soft strokes. He pulled back slowly.

"Wow..." his voice was husky. Tory was still paralyzed. Her eyes just fluttered.

"Will you come home with me?" He whispered.

"Yes." She didn't even hesitate.

CHAPTER 5

"I don't live that far from here; about three blocks, but if you want I can call us a cab-"

"I think that I can manage three blocks."

"You can, but how are your feet?"

"If you were serious about that foot massage then I think there's incentive." He grinned and stood, slipping on his jacket before taking her hand.

Once they got out to the night air, he placed his hand around her waist and she did the same. She sighed in contentment as they walked arm in arm.

"How old are you?" She asked, seemingly out of the blue. He gave her a surprised look.

"I'm sorry, I'm thirty three. I should have mentioned that. Second to the youngest in my family." They walked at a comfortable pace. Her feet were screaming at her but she didn't limp much. With his arms around her, it seemed that her feet barely touched the ground!

They reached a crosswalk with a red light and Lee's hand very slowly moved to cup her rear as they waited for the light to change. She'd never done anything like this before, but her hand slipped down and she palmed his tight ass.

"And all this time I thought you were a shy girl." He smiled. Damn, that smile could melt a block of ice!

"Come here..." She pulled his head boldly down to hers and her lips crushed against his. She heard the bell tone of the light indicating for them to walk. They stood there on the corner kissing instead.

"Tory, you better be careful," he groaned. "I haven't kissed like this in a long time and I might be forced to skip your foot rub...for something better."

"To hell with the foot rub," she said boldly and pulled his ass until his pelvis was flush with her belly. She sighed in pleasure when hardness met her soft belly. Lee's hands suddenly gripped her ass, holding her in place as his pelvis rolled against her, knees dipping slightly as he thrust forward.

"Mmm..." Tory whimpered as the center of her leaped in response. The stop light indicator sounded again and this time Lee tore himself away from her. He gripped her hand and pulled her across the street at a fast walk. When he got to the curb he took it slowly and waited for her to step up. He again pulled her along, walking briskly.

"Come on baby, two more blocks."

"Ok!" She laughed as she clipped along after him. She was starting to pant.

Lee groaned. "Ohhhh, baby," he half joked. "You sound so sexy!"

Tory laughed and for once was happy to allow herself to become breathless. They reached another corner but they had the light so Lee led her across quickly without pausing.

"Lee..." she panted, "If it's much further-"

"No, we're here. It's the third building up." He led her to the entrance of a large building but instead of guiding her up the stairs to go inside he embraced her, stroking her back, giving her an opportunity to catch her breath. She rested her head on his big chest until her breathing calmed.

After a few moments he looked down at her. "Ready?"

She nodded against him. "Please tell me you have an elevator."

"Yes." He kissed her nose. "It's pretty rickety inside so be careful."

Now her feet were in serious jeopardy of giving out on her as she took the stairs. "It's dark." She said, gripping his arm as they entered the building.

"I know. I'm the only person in the building so I usually keep the light off." He put his arm around her. "Don't worry, I'll guide you." Tory thought that this evening had been full of wonder...but being led through a darkened building by a blind man had to be the kicker.

Lee pulled up the gate of an industrial sized elevator. He helped her in and soundly closed it. At least in here was an emergency light that cast a soft glow over the harsh, unfinished building interior.

"This is kind of a work in progress. I'm the first tenant so excuse the mess. I told them that I didn't mind as long as they kept the walkway clear." The lift came to a jerky stop, but his arms held her in reassurance as he reached up with the other to lift open the gate. "The elevator is perfectly safe. The door to the loft won't open unless the gate is in place."

They stepped into the darkened room and this time Lee reached over to hit the lights.

"Oh my God..." Tory's hands went to her mouth. The loft was gorgeous! He led her into the oversized room. The ceilings had to be fifteen feet! It was immaculate with tiled or stone floors that indicated the separation of rooms instead of walls. This was nothing like the cold cement floors and brick walls that she would see in the movies. This was a successful man's home. It had obviously been professionally decorated. She eyed Lee curiously.

He had money like that?

"Do you like it? They gave it to me already furnished. Cost more...but it's not like I could have done anything like this." It was decorated very minimalist, which didn't mean that it was cold and emotionless. It was very much the opposite. There were wooden carvings and art on the walls that had texture. The windows were floor to ceiling and sheathed in blinds that when drawn showed an oriental design.

A cat leaped from a perch and strutted over to investigate the visitor. The orange tabby blinked at her and then circled her legs with a slight purr.

"Hey kitty." Tory reached down and stroked the cat's back. "What's your cat's name?"

"I haven't named her yet. I found her when I moved here. But she answers to cat...or the sound of a can of cat food opening." He moved toward the kitchen. "I figured she could work off her room board by catching mice and keeping me company. Would you like something to drink?"

"Yes, thanks."

"Soda, iced tea, beer, wine-?"

"Water is fine."

"Really? That's all?"

"Yes. Do you mind if I freshen up a bit?" he pointed.

"Behind that glass block wall." As she headed in the direction that he'd indicated, he called out again. "You'll find towels and washcloths in the pantry. Take your time, baby."

Baby...she grinned at the use of that word. It didn't sound cheesy coming out of his mouth, either. His accent made it sound very sexy.

The bathroom was a dream. She resisted the urge to snoop and located a washcloth and removed her makeup and freshened up. She'd done a lot of sweating between dancing and the quick walk.

She returned to the living room to see that Lee had dimmed the lights and that soft music was playing across his sound system. His electronic equipment alone probably cost more than half a year of her salary!

He heard her coming and held out his hand to her. She took it with no hesitation. He led her to the couch where her bottled water sat on the nearby cocktail table.

"Have a seat. I'll be right back." He headed in the direction that she had come and Tory opened the bottled water, drinking long and leaning back against the cushions of the large couch. She sighed in contentment. How had she gotten from watching a sexy man on the bus to sitting in his expensive loft? She resisted the urge to pinch herself.

He returned, walking into the living room without hesitation and navigating with no problems. He sat down on the couch next to her and patted his lap. At first she thought that he wanted her sitting on his lap, which she would have done without thought.

"Take off your shoes and let me rub those feet of yours. Put them up here."

Tory sat up and placed her drink back on the table. "Can you...just kiss me again?" She remembered the feel of him hard, pressing against her, and her breath strained to reach her lungs.

"*Anda cá...*" He whispered. Come here...

Tory slid across the couch and his hand found her thigh. His lips moved to her neck and he lightly nibbled a trail down to her shoulder. She let her head fall back, feeling dizzy from his attention. She slid her hand into the curls of his hair. He nipped the mound of her breast, capturing the flesh lightly between his teeth and causing Tory to moan.

His hands moved up to cup her breasts, thumbs seeking out her nipples and upon finding their slight impression within her bra, he rubbed his thumbs over the cloth and through to her sensitized flesh.

"Oh...yes..." She clutched at his arms, holding him there, or hanging on--she wasn't sure which. His lips moved up to her mouth and he plunged his tongue into her, searching for her tongue and sucking it sensually.

Tory's heart was pounding in her chest. She'd never experienced sensations like these. She hardly knew what to do with her hands; her body. He was so much more experienced than she.

He'd at least done this before! She wanted to do something that would make him moan; to set him on the verge of exploding.

Tory drew her fingers down his taut belly and felt him flinch as a gust of air left his body. Ahhh...so she had found his spot. His kissing became more aggressive and she moved her hand up his body and found his flat areola with its puckered little nipple. She gently rolled it through the thin material, and Lee shuddered.

"*Isso sabe muito bem...*" He murmured. She figured that if all of his senses were heightened...then touch would be as well, and she was right. Tory moved her hands around his body, pulling up the fabric of his t-shirt, exposing the taut muscles of his stomach. Her hands moved lightly grazing him there and she felt his muscles quiver. He pulled back from her kiss, surprised. He smiled slightly

"What are you doing to me, *querida*? That feels amazing..."

She leaned in to kiss him again. "I want to make you feel as good as you are making me feel."

"Yes..." He returned the kiss with fervor, slipping his tongue into her mouth. Not having much experience in frenching, Tory just followed his lead, doing everything that he did but only half a second after.

His lips travelled down her neck, over her shoulder and then to the mound of her breast.

'I can't believe this is happening!' Tory thought when his hands brushed the material of her summer dress from her shoulders revealing her lacy black bra. He positioned his hands beneath each Double D bra cup, testing the weight. He seemed pleased. She strained to see his lips as they moved over her brown skin. He dragged down the delicate material of her bra exposing her nipples. He eagerly gathered one into his mouth.

"Oh...God..." She groaned, which only caused him to increase his attention to her puckered nipple. He pressed his fingertips lightly against the other causing a jolt of electrical-like energy to zip between her clenched thighs.

"Lee!" She sat up suddenly, causing him to rise up and give her a questioning look. "I've...I've never done this before."

His face took on a look of awe as he considered her. He sat back suddenly. "You're a virgin?"

She sat up as well, embarrassed that he was looking at her--or staring at her like she was a freak. She quickly pulled her clothes straight to conceal herself.

"Well...I've never made love but no, I'm not a virgin." Revealing this caused her to look down.

He didn't speak for a long time. "It would be my pleasure to make love to you for the first time when you're ready. If not tonight-"

"Oh, I'm ready." She spoke quickly. "I just wanted you to know that I'm not...experienced."

He didn't speak immediately, and when he did it was a whisper. "I think that I will fall madly in love with you, *querida*."

"Oh." She swallowed past the lump that had formed in her throat. "I think I'd like that, Lee. I'd like that very much." He offered her his hand and she took it—his fingers gently enclosing hers. He turned and led her across the room. They rounded the glass block and ended up in the bedroom. His king size bed was the focal point of the entire room; sheathed in a bright red satin comforter, the only illumination coming from the living area of the house, which gave it a surreal feel.

'*This is the bed where I will lose my virginity...*' Tory thought. That thought sent her quaking in fear. She wanted this; more than anything that she could imagine, but it was the culmination of all of her fantasies coming to fruition; and it was overwhelming.

He turned to her, still holding her hand. "Are you ok?"

"Just anxious."

He rubbed her arms gently. "We don't have to-"

Tory boldly gripped his muscular ass, pulling him to her. He seemed genuinely surprised but also pleased to allow her to take control. She moved her hands to his body, running them over his muscles, before yanking up his shirt and pulling it over his head. He helped her to remove it, allowing it to drop on the floor.

"Oh..." Tory moaned as she took in his perfectly sculptured form; not too big and not too small. Her hands moved over his naked chest her eyes unable to ignore the obvious contrast in their skin color. She allowed her finger to graze his nipple. Her hand was dark against his much paler skin and she instantly thought of the ying yang symbol.

He had been patient in waiting for her to make the next move, but when her fingers circled his areola, Lee began to shudder. His reaction made her even bolder. She closed the slight space between them, hands sliding up the muscular mound of his ass. Her hands then slipped down the back of pants, connecting with his naked buttocks.

"Mmmm, Tory..." He sighed in a husky voice. Immediately, he placed his hands on her ample bottom. His hooded eyes appeared as slashes in his face as he enjoyed the feel of her curves. "Oooo. You are teasing me relentlessly. And here I thought you were a good girl. I see that you know how to be very bad." She placed her mouth on his nipple; first one then the other and he gasped. "Ahh!" She looked up with a twinkle in her eye. Yes, that was the reaction she was going for.

"Is this too much for you? I can stop. We can just hold each other-" she joked.

A passionate growl issued from him and he pressed his lips to hers. He reclaimed his control when he lifted her bodily in his arms and walked to the bed. He slowly and carefully placed her on top of the comforter. And then he unfastened his pants as she stared up at him. He paused. You can look at me naked, but only if I can look at you. Is that a deal?"

She let out a brave sigh. "Yes. I can do that." She stood slowly and the both of them stripped out of their clothing. Lee was much quicker and was standing before her with a firm body that was every bit as impressive as the statue of David. His erection was thick enough to cause her heart to pound again fearfully. When she had shed everything except her panties and bra, she took a brave breath and removed those last two items, tossing them across the room where they landed on a nearby chair.

He reached for her, hands gliding over her; each curve, each fold, each stretch mark... '*What is he thinking?*' she wondered. And then she saw that he was even harder than before! He climbed onto the bed and she followed him.

Tory lay down, now more turned-on than nervous. When his hands touched her again, she began to feel as beautiful as he seemed to think she was. Again, Lee took the time to explore her body with his hands, and then soon he used his lips and lastly he used his tongue. She was a bundle of nerves so that soon, even when he leaned over her, Tory shivered uncontrollably.

When he traced the line of her most intimate crease with one fingertip she moaned softly, parting her legs, exposing her swollen nub. He leaned forward and kissed it. Her body jerked in response. He parted her with two fingers and then sucked her into his mouth.

Tory arched her back and moaned. Her legs began to tremble violently when he lapped at her pussy with long, hard strokes. Tory reached down and gripped his head, more roughly then she realized but Lee didn't complain. She screeched loudly, fists buried in his silky curls, body thrashing as his tongue worked her hungrily. He paused and reached up, gripping her wrists and removing her death grip from his hair. Her body relaxed instantly and she panted for breath. Lee slid from the bed, moving to the side table where he retrieved a condom.

Seeing him so hard and ready right there, inches from her face, Tory reached out and wrapped her hand around his shaft while he was preoccupied with the condom. He gasped in surprise and then growled something in Portuguese. Quicker than ever, he had the prophylactic out of its wrapper. Yet, instead of rolling it on, he closed his eyes and allowed Tory's fingers to explore him. He felt like satin. Her fingers traced the veins, reveling at how hard a man could get. She circled the head of his engorged cock and Lee could bear no more. He quickly positioned the condom and then moved to nestle between Tory's thighs. She spread her legs wide for him and then felt him push gently into her.

She tensed when the parting of her flesh became painful.

"Okay?" He paused, not advancing. She nodded, biting her lips. He kissed her, lingering into it until her heart began to pitter patter again and her hips rolled beneath him. He pushed into her again, slowly, withdrawing a bit and then pressing forward until little by little he was completely within her. He cupped her full breast and listened intently for signs of her pleasure.

Tory closed her eyes and concentrated on the steady rhythm of Lee's hips; entering, withdrawing, entering, withdrawing. Her chest suddenly hitched and she groaned. It was the sound Lee was waiting for. He continued stoking the fires within her, listening to her breath as it came in gasps, the quivering of her muscles, the movement of her hips. He increased the tempo and she cried out; not in pain but in pleasure.

"*Acertei? É este o ponto certo?* Yes! Come on, baby!"

She continued groaning, moving her hips to match his, feeling the electricity spiraling out from her core, and then cried out loudly as a sudden explosion of pleasure engulfed her.

Her body clenched down and Lee sucked in a soft breath. "Oh my God..." He felt lightheaded when he finally allowed his body's release. It took every bit of his control not to thrust roughly with abandon! He knew he would hurt her and that one thought kept his pace steady even when his toes clenched in orgasm.

Tory's body moved in ways that she never thought she could do without blushing and she called out sounds that would have embarrassed her before tonight. But the pleasure of her first man induced orgasm took all thought away...all thought but one, and that was the feel of Lee's engorged penis moving rapidly in and out of her.

When his movements became staccato and the last cry of pleasure sounded loudly through the loft, Lee and Tory lay panting in each other's arms.

He held her, whispering softly in Portuguese. She didn't know what he said but it didn't matter. She would listen to him speak in this way to her for as long as he wanted to do it.

CHAPTER 6

Tory's eyes popped open but she didn't immediately move. She was under the covers of a bed more comfortable then hers ever had been and an arm was draped over her belly; the body it connected to spooned behind her. But that was not the reason for the slight frown that creased her brow.

What had awakened her was the mechanical sound of the elevator from the other side of the large home. Lee was sleeping, she could tell by the loud, steady sound of his breathing. Who was coming up the elevator? Should she wake him?

The gate came up. It wasn't so loud that it should wake Lee up, but since this wasn't her home, any strange noise was alarming to her. By the pinkish light coming through the slats of the window it was just daybreak...seven am?

She wanted to jump up and put her clothes on...but then she didn't want to leave the safety of the bed; nor the concealment of the comforter. She finally shook Lee's arm.

"Lee!" She whispered.

"Mmm?" He sighed, still half asleep.

"Sweetie, there's somebody in the loft."

His eyes came open slowly and he stretched, lazily, becoming oriented. "Oh, that's Rosalind."

Rosalind? The hostess from the restaurant? She gave him a curious look, waiting for an explanation. Of course he couldn't see the look. He gave her a quick squeeze, pulling her into his arms.

"Does two people with morning breath cancel each other out?" He asked.

Her brow was knit in alarm that Rosalind was in the house. "No." She said seriously.

"Okay, then we'll save the good morning kiss for later." He sat up in bed with the comforter over his lap. "Honey? What did I do with my underwear?"

Honey. He called her honey. She suppressed a smile. "They are...at ten o'clock." She whispered even though he was talking in a normal voice. She had the comforter clutched to her breast, all the way up to her neck. He stood up and stretched again.

Momentarily she forgot about the girl in the other room and appraised his rounded ass and the line of his back that tapered down to a narrow waist. Damn...no; DAYUM!!!

She shook her head and quickly smoothed down her hair. Lee used his feet to find his undies and slipped them on quickly. "Stay there, I'll get your clothes."

"My...panties and bra are on the chair." She whispered. He found them and handed them to her and she climbed beneath the comforter to pull them on frantically. She was hoping to be at least partially dressed before Rosalind made her appearance; but no such luck.

"*Hey, o que é que fazes aqui?*" She rounded the glass block and froze in her spot at the sight of Tory peeking out from beneath the comforter. The Portuguese woman's face was in complete shock and her mouth formed a large O.

"Getting dressed." Lee was fastening his pants. "Roz, we'll be right out."

"Oh my God! I'm so sorry!" She scurried out of the room. Lee reached down and felt for Tory's dress. She took it from him in embarrassment. What was that woman doing just walking into a grown man's bedroom? He was only seconds from being butt naked!

"Roz comes by on Saturdays to help me with some errands and things; grocery shopping and such." At seven am???

"Why so early?"

"Well to get it out of the way. She's got kids and a hubby." When she was all dressed, Lee reached for her hand. "And when she's not helping me with errands then one of my brothers and sisters do. I don't need much help; I do my own chores, laundry etc."

When they reached the living room, Rosalind was busily opening the drapes. Tory saw that she'd disposed of the two containers of bottled water. The woman looked at her and Tory saw the recognition. Roz's eyes did a quick scan of her disheveled form before giving her a worried look.

"I'm so sorry, I-he's usually alone."

"Roz, this is Tory." Lee seemed not the least affected by the fact that both women were uncomfortable.

"I remember, from the restaurant." She hurried over and offered her hand. Roz was pretty, appearing to be in her early thirties. She was tall, probably five ten, but her height did a lot to counteract her weight. She was a big woman but also statuesque one.

The two women clasped hands and as Lee moved towards the kitchen Tory hurried to the couch where her purse still sat and her shoes lay on the floor.

"Hon, do you want coffee?" Lee called.

"Yes." Both women replied in unison. They stared at each other suddenly.

"Three coffees coming up."

Tory focused on putting on her shoes...damned feet had swollen and they didn't want to go on easily.

"So..." Roz stood there with her arms crossed before her. "You and Lee are...together?"

"Uhm..." She hadn't thought that far.

"The reason I ask is because your shoes were on the floor." She gave Tory a steady look. "And this is the path that he walks. This is the type of thing that could cause him a serious injury...something as small as a carelessly strewn shoe."

Tory's mouth opened and then closed. She was embarrassed and wasn't sure what to say. "I'll keep that in mind."

Roz watched her, seeming to want to say more but instead she turned and went to the kitchen. Wow, no one had ever dismissed her so completely. Tory limped to the bathroom and quickly had a meltdown at the sight of her hair. She put it in some order with the items in her bag and then she washed her face and found mouthwash to gurgle with. She didn't like facing someone who obviously didn't like her, while wearing day old panties and having bed head, but she had no choice.

She walked back to the living room bravely and Lee called out to her from the kitchen. "Tory, we're in here."

The kitchen was open, a bar and stools defining the space. Yet off to the side was a small dining area near two large windows that overlooked the city. A walk out balcony was nearby. This was just...awesome.

"How do you take your coffee, Babe?" Tory resisted the urge to glance at Roz to see if she'd answer, but the woman was already sipping her drink.

"Cream and sugar."

"Non dairy creamer, ok?"

"Perfect."

He poured her coffee carefully and then passed it to her. The cream and sugar he placed on the breakfast bar, and then last a spoon from a drawer.

"I was telling Roz about Club Kat last night. The music was HOT! Didn't you like that band, Baby?"

"Yeah, I'm new to Reggaeton but I definitely like it."

"Tory, honey, you have to have a Portuguese rib the way you danced!"

Roz laughed in a joking way. "Lee you don't have a Latin girl you have a black one. Man I know you're blind, but you're not that blind are you?!"

Lee considered his coffee, sipping without comment. Tory blinked. He did know that she was black??? He'd touched her hair...it was relaxed but...

Lee suddenly turned and poured his coffee down the drain. "Tory, we'll take you home. Is that okay, Roz?

"Roz was still chuckling. "Of course." Her eyes locked on Tory's before she gave one last laugh.

"I'm going to shower real quick." He said as he left the kitchen. "I won't be long."

When Lee was gone, Roz stood and moved about the kitchen, putting everything back in its place. The Portuguese woman ignored her and Tory quickly stood and went into the living room, feeling self-conscious. She could hear the shower going in the bathroom and the movements of Roz in the kitchen.

Feeling awkward, Tory quickly picked up her things intending to slip out of the apartment. She didn't care if she looked a hot mess and smelled of sex. She was going to catch the bus and go home. She was uncomfortable and it wasn't all because of Roz, something about Lee's reactions made her feel unsure. She didn't know what was up with him but she wanted to be gone.

She was just reaching out to press the button for the elevator when she paused. She closed her eyes and bit her lips, recalling the fun they'd had at the club; and then after. No, she wasn't going to run away like she had before. She marched to the bathroom and knocked on the closed door.

"Yeah?" Came his voice.

She opened the door and slipped into the bathroom, closing it behind her. "Um...I think I'm going to pass on the ride home. My bus stop isn't far and-"

"Roz makes you uncomfortable?" The water turned off and he pulled back the shower curtain. He reached for a towel and Tory's breath caught in her throat. She was supposed to be saying something but for the life of her she couldn't recollect what...He was gorgeous standing there with water streaming down his toned body as he quickly dried.

"Tory?"

"Oh, um, I don't think she likes me very much." And you act like you're trying to get rid of me...

Lee wrapped the towel around his waist and gestured to her. "Come here, honey." She walked to him slowly. He had a serious expression on his face. She stopped walking when she was a mere foot from him. He placed his hands around her shapely body.

"I've known Roz since I was a kid. She's like family. For a moment I forgot that you don't know her like that. I could tell that you were really uncomfortable. If you don't want Roz to drive you home then that's fine. But I...don't want our day to end."

"You don't? I thought you wanted me to go."

His brow arched. "I know your feet are sore. When I was lying in bed last night...I wished that I could drive you home and then I hoped you'd let me call you a cab. When she came over I thought it would be perfect...I just didn't want you walking to the bus stop, is all. Okay? I don't want you to leave. As a matter of fact..." He stepped closer to her. "I'd like to keep you here for a few more hours." His hands moved to her bottom and rubbed her softly. "Tory?"

"Hmmm?" She was staring deeply into his sexy hooded eyes.

"Does two coffee breaths cancel each other out?" His lips were a mere inch from hers.

"Kiss me and let's find out." She muttered and then he kissed her softly. Her hands moved to his shoulders, still wet from his shower, and then up to his dripping curls. Lee pulled her tight against his body, his fingers caressing her full rear end.

She pulled back suddenly. "Lee?"

He blinked. "What?"

"You did know that I'm black, before your friend told you, right?"

"Yeah," he shrugged. "I could tell that you were black. And later when I asked Macey what you looked like she told me that you were a light skinned black woman with a voluptuous body and a gorgeous face. Also, that you were a big tipper." He added the last with a grin.

Tory blushed. "Gorgeous? Your sister honestly said that?"

He placed his hand over his heart. "Cross my heart. That's what she said."

Tory smiled. "Lee, maybe we should get out of the bathroom."

He sighed. "I guess you're right." He refastened his towel. "Do you want to go shopping with us?" He asked hopefully. "Don't let Roz make you uncomfortable. She's just very protective of me, is all. We've been friends forever and she knows how it's been for me with girlfriends."

Girlfriends. Did he mean girlfriend or friend that is a girl? She looked at the sexy man. She wanted to say, 'hell no.' She didn't want to go shopping with *them*. She wanted to go shopping with HIM. But she wasn't ready to say goodbye to him yet, either. Plus it would probably aggravate that Roz to no end if she tagged along.

"Well I have to shower and change-" He was already moving past her to turn the shower back on. "Shower here, then put your clothes back on, and we'll get you back to your place, then you can change. How's that--? Oh, and put on some walking shoes!"

She laughed. "I can't shower here! My hair-" He pulled off his towel.

"Come. Shower with me, *querida*."

She sucked in a long breath. "Okay." Quickly, she pulled off her clothes and they entered the shower together. He grabbed the soap before she could and began washing her body. She would have been timid about it, had it not been for his obvious show of 'happiness' as his hands explored her soapy flesh.

He groaned. "*Tu és tão linda...*" His mouth lowered to her breasts and he drew one nipple, then the other into his mouth, suckling gently. She winced as the pleasure engulfed her, groaning as quietly as she could manage. Her hand slid between them and she wrapped her fingers around his thick shaft.

Lee shuddered and he moved to enter her, but she pulled out of his grip and sank down to her knees, no longer worried about the water soaking her hair. She tentatively kissed the tip of his swollen cock head.

He cried out, body jerking. "Tory..." His fingers slid lightly into her wet hair as he threw his head back. She could see his adam's apple bobbing as he repeatedly gulped. She had always wondered what it would be like to place a man into her mouth. It was the man that made it feel wonderful; because Lee's groans and shivers broadcast each stroke of her tongue. It was obvious that she was bringing him great pleasure and that alone brought her pleasure.

She was tentative at first, carefully lapping, and kissing and sucking just the head. But his moans encouraged her to be more daring and she slipped her mouth over his length until he was almost at the back of her throat. Suddenly she gagged, almost choking.

He was breathing hard, trying not to move, trying not to cause her to choke again and she remembered her brief experimentation with purging. She only gagged when her finger touched the back of her tongue. She sucked him again, this time running the tip of him along the roof of her mouth and down her throat.

"Oh, Torrrrryy!" He called out her name. She couldn't believe it, but she was deep throating! She felt his fingers turn into fists in her hair as he tried to control himself. She sucked and bobbed her head over him, swallowing the tantalizing mixture of saliva, precum and water from the shower.

"I'm going to cum!" He cried out. He tried to pull from her mouth but she wanted to taste him and wouldn't allow it. The first creamy spurts shot down her throat and she did gag again. But then she released him enough to grip his shaft in her fist, working him until the last drop had spilled from him. She stroked his tight scrotum once and he gasped and jerked.

"Oh my God..." He helped her to stand. "Oh Baby..." He was breathless as he held on to her.

"I take it, I did it right?"

He nodded silently. He suddenly reached up and put his hand on her cheek. "Tory...I think that we get along really good. And I love being with you—not just like this, but just talking to you and dancing and...well, I do like this too."

She smiled.

"I want to be with you, all the time; a couple. I know we haven't known each other long, but-""I was hoping you'd want that. I've been watching you just like you've been watching me. I thought..." she hesitated and plunged forward, "I thought that's all there would ever be, watching and wishing."

He kissed her. "I've watched you for a long time, Tory, waiting each day for you to get on the bus, wondering what you think of me and how I would approach you. And days when I don't get to see you then I'm disappointed. You never have to worry about how I feel about you. I'll always show you my feelings."

They touched foreheads murmuring their feelings until there was a loud rapping on the bathroom door.

"*Vocês vão passar o dia todo aí?!*" Came Roz's tight, angry voice.

Lee grimaced in embarrassment. "*Desculpa! Já estamos a sair!*"

"*É que eu tenho mais que fazer hoje!*"

"*Desculpa! Desculpa!*" Lee reached up and turned off the shower. "We better get out there."

Tory gave him a curious look wondering what was said. She was not going to like this whole

91

thing of speaking Portuguese unless it was Lee speaking sexy words to her. He got her a fresh towel and then quickly dried himself, rubbing his hair briskly before heading for the door. He wrapped the towel snuggly around his waist, pausing before reaching for the door knob.

"Ready?" She had already pulled on her clothes again and was just wrapping the towel around her sopping wet hair. Man was she ever a mess...but it had been worth it.

She grinned. "Yep, ready."

He opened the door and they quickly hurried to the bedroom but Tory still saw Roz sprawled on the couch looking pissed to high hell.

CHAPTER 7

Lee dressed quickly in cargo pants and a T-shirt that made her want to strip him down and jump his bones. She dug into her purse and retrieved her hairbrush and hairpins and made a cute bun out of her wet, ruined hair. She put on a bit of lipstick and then they went out to the living room together holding hands.

Roz looked at her watch. "Let's go if we're going. We're dropping you off, right...um...what's your name?"

"Actually I'm going with you. Lee invited me shopping."

"She's Tory." Lee reminded her while guiding them to the elevator.

Tory looked down at her clothes. "I still need to go home and change, though. Can't shop in dancing shoes!"

Roz gave her a brief, unfriendly look as Lee closed them into the elevator and pressed the controls.

Although it wasn't normally Tory's nature she couldn't help but to get in the other woman's face just a little. "I suppose since Lee and I are a couple now I should probably learn all of the things that you do for him—so that you won't have to do it anymore." Lee squeezed her, and the way he did it, she could tell that he knew exactly what she was doing and was giving his approval.

"A couple?" Roz's voice was low. "I thought you just met..."

The elevator stopped at the first floor and Lee opened the doors and ushered them out.

"I watched her for a while. And I know for a fact that she's a keeper. Tory is the perfect mix of sweetness, innocence and woman. I was really lucky to have met her and I won't be letting her get away." Tory forgot about Roz then as she looked up at her man...Mmmm...her man. She put her hand through his arm and became his cane. Roz looked on stiffly.

She finally plastered on a fake smile as they walked to where her car was parked at the curb. "Well, I should show her the ropes of leading the blind."

"Well, she's pretty damn good. She's been my cane for a couple days now."

"Well that's places that you already know. She hasn't helped you in a new place." Roz spoke defensively.

"My place is new." He looked at her and smiled.

Back at her home, Tory led Lee into her apartment while Roz trailed them--checking out everything with a critical eye. Well, she knew that she was a bit quirky. She liked vintage movie posters, and antique furniture that didn't match but had beautiful fabric or great texture. She had knickknacks that weren't all-together cute, but that meant something special to her; like the cloth voodoo doll that sat on her bookshelf, given to her by her paternal grandmother. There was the elaborate candelabra that looked straight out of a Frankenstein movie, but a piece that she absolutely had not been able to take her eyes from when she saw it in an antique shop. It was huge and overbearing in her small dining area but she didn't care because she loved it!

Lee removed his cane from one of the pockets of his cargo pants. She hadn't even seen him stow it there. She looked around quickly, eyes darting at the likely hazards in his path. He might bump into the CD/DVD holder, the arms of the entertainment center stuck out and would need to be folded back, you had to squeeze past the couch and chair in order to get into the dining room..."Go and get changed." Roz said while taking Lee's other arm. "I'll take it from here." Tory hesitated and then leaned in quickly to kiss Lee's cheek. She hurriedly changed into jeans and a casual blouse. Lastly she laced up tennis shoes and hurried back into the living room after checking herself in the mirror.

She didn't look too bad considering that she had just recently resembled a drowned rat.

As she re-entered the room, she overheard Roz talking. "Be careful here. There's a rug. It's old and curled on the ends." Tory blushed in embarrassment. It was an old rug but it was a clean one. She cleared her throat.

"Okay, I'm ready. Shall we go?"

Lee was touching a small metal bell, running his fingers over its surface. He quickly returned it to the mantle.

"I like your apartment." He said breathlessly. "There's a lot to see. I can't wait until you show me everything." Tory was about to smile when Roz decided to open her mouth.

"Yeah, well this place is an accident waiting to happen."

Lee tilted his head, turning in her direction. "Rosalind."

"It's a...cute apartment but this clutter is going to cause you to trip over something and break your neck! This place is *é uma bagunça.* And that's being nice." She gave a distasteful look around. *"Não é lá muito limpo!"*

"Rosalind!" Lee spoke sharply.

Tory looked from one to the other. "What did you?" Rosalind crossed her arms in front of her without responding. Tory turned to Lee. "Lee, what did she just say?"

"Tory...nothing. Let's just-"

"I want to know what she said!" She snapped finally reaching her breaking point with the two of them speaking secretly to each other just because they knew a different language and she didn't.

Lee turned to Rosalind. "Roz...you need to just leave."

Tory stomped her foot and brought her hands together sharply. "No! I'm not having this. You two are not going to be speaking over my head. I want to know what she said and I want to know NOW!"

Roz was breathing hard. It was obvious that she wanted to do battle with the younger, woman. And yet she wouldn't until she got some indication from Lee what would happen next.

Lee scowled. "She said that your house is dirty. *Tens que pedir desculpa!*" He seemed to suddenly remember to speak English and amended. "Rosalind, you're going to apologize to her this instant and then you're going to leave!"

Tory was speechless. Her apartment was cluttered, maybe a bit dusty but it was not dirty! She felt like defending herself but wouldn't. She wasn't dirty. She rubbed her elbows. She was not a dirty person.

"Lee, don't be silly. I'm not going to just leave you here. I've never left you someplace in my entire life and I'm not going to star-"

"I don't know what your damn problem is! But you've gone out of your way to be rude to my girlfriend." His voice was so angry that it shook. "What is wrong with you?"

Tory finally found her voice "I can't...believe what you just said." Her eyes narrowed. "How dare you call my apartment dirty!" She had never been so insulted! She'd had to fight for years to feel clean and here was some woman implying that she wasn't. She started shaking with sudden rage.

"I know what your real problem is." Tory spat. "You want Lee. You want him—and not as a family friend, not as a brother. He may not be able to see how you look at him, but I do! Am I right, Rosalind? You want him the way a woman wants a lover! "

"You're sick!" Roz said. "Lee, let's get out of here!"

Lee reached out his hands and Roz took them. He yanked away from her. "Tory?" She brushed past Rosalind and gave Lee her hands. Then she glared at the woman who no longer held a superior look on her face, who now looked scared and filled with anguish.

"The novelty is going to run out for her, just like it did for all of the others-"

"Don't do this here-" he said.

"Family will be here when she isn't! I'll be here, like I've always been here."

He scratched his head. "Roz...you're married. You have the boys. I mean-that was a long time ago. We were just kids and...*you* ended that."

"I was stupid. I was young and stupid. I thought that the world was my oyster, Lee. I didn't know what I had in you until I went out there and everyone else was-"

"Don't!" He said. He rubbed his face and Tory watched. He hadn't known. He honestly hadn't known...but now that he did, would he want her? They obviously had history.

Lee blew out a loud voice. "Roz...you're like a sister to me. I mean, we were like fourteen years old. I was broken hearted when you dumped me but I got over it."

"But...I haven't."

"Roz...I met someone that I really like. I'm sorry but...I don't feel that way about you."

Roz looked at Tory, not with anger, but with so much hurt and pain that she almost felt it herself. It was the hurt that she'd felt more than once in her life when she wanted a man and she knew that he wouldn't want her...not ever. But for Roz it was a hundred times over.

"I'm sorry," she choked out and then hurried out of the apartment.

Tory was silent for a moment. "Do you want to go after her?"

"No," he said firmly. "I'm here with you." He gripped her fingertips and pulled her into his arms. "I'm so sorry. There's enough baggage without that-"

"Shh!" She kissed him lightly. "I don't think that about you at all."

He frowned. "Are you sure? If this ever gets too much-"

"Lee."

"No. If it does I'd rather you walk away then just stay with me out of guilt. If I start thinking that..."She kissed him again. "I guess you have to say that, huh? But the same thing goes for you. If you don't want me anymore-"

He sighed. "Unless you turn into a maniac over night, I don't see that happening...and even if that did happen, it'd be hard to let you go. I'd have to get a long chain and keep all sharp instruments away from you." She giggled and then grew serious.

"You didn't get your shopping done."

He smiled. "I can do my shopping alone. I just call up there and the grocery store that I shop at gets one of the baggers to guide me. Of course, it's more convenient when I have someone with a car for the bigger stuff like litter for Cat, or bottled water. But truthfully, sweetheart, I am very self-sufficient. Do you know what the ACCESS bus is?"

"I've seen that." She'd seen handicapped people using it.

He nodded. "They take me to and from my appointments when it's not convenient for me to take the metro or when my family isn't available." His eyes crinkled a bit. "I do have one problem though; when I'm in a lovely lady's apartment and I find that I've skipped breakfast and am ravenously hungry. We should do something for breakfast...or is it lunch now?"

"Oh, yeah, I'm starving myself. What we had yesterday was interesting but not a meal."

"True." He gripped her butt. "We can't go having you dropping weight and losing this booty that I love so much."

She laughed. "Did you just say booty?"

"I was going to say ass but I didn't want to be crass."

"Mmmm." She kissed him again and then pulled out of his grip. "Okay." She gripped his hand. "I'm going to lead you to the kitchen, but there are a lot of things to see along the way so it might take a while."

He nodded happily and had an expression as if he was about to open presents at Christmas.

It took nearly half an hour before they finally reached the kitchen. He touched each knickknack and each knickknack held an interesting story. He listened intently as she described a rock that her mother had found on a beach in Florida, where she and her Dad had moved. There was a photograph of the three of them during a happier time and even though he couldn't see the photograph she described it for him. She placed a kewpie doll in his hand and he tilted his head in confusion at the ghoulish figure. Her Daddy had bought it for her and she loved it dearly. She finally let him 'look' a chipped porcelain pig that she purchased out of a sense of kinship.

Eventually reaching the kitchen, she decided to show him what magic she could do in here. She made a huge frittata omelet with potatoes and cheese, bacon, peppers and onions. He had two servings. As they ate, they talked mainly about her; about her being an only child and her parents living down in Florida now and how much she missed them.

"You seemed really happy when you were a kid."

"I was."

"But not so much now." He observed. "What changed?"

Her face fell. She wasn't sure if she wanted to talk about that yet. She pushed the subject into a different direction. "Well, it's just that being a fat woman in our society is tough."

"It seems that the worst of it is that it makes you feel as if you are less. When actually, I think you're perfect the way you are. But what matters is not what I think, but what you think."

"I think that I'm overweight. But I don't think that I would have been an unhappy fat woman if it wasn't for the way people look at me." He nodded and reached for her hand.

"You know that I don't dislike your weight. I like you — all of you."

"I know you mean that."

He sighed. "I think I'm ready to take a tour of the bathroom." She laughed and left him at the bathroom door to explore it all on his own.

"Tory." He called when he was finished. She was in the kitchen cleaning up. He was making his way down the short hall using his cane.

"I'm here."

"I want you to take me to the bus stop."

"What?"

"I want you to take me the route that you walk every morning...or should I say run?"

"I'm never going to live that down."

"You got a bus schedule? I'm going to take you out on the town, love."

"Oh?" She grabbed her purse and keys then searched for her bus schedule. When they had everything, she looped her arm around his and led him out the door. He didn't put away his cane and seemed to concentrate more, yet he was still talkative and asked her questions about her neighborhood. It only took them five minutes to get to the bus stop which was only around the block from her home.

He turned to her seriously. "I can come visit you Tory. This is very simple to navigate." She looked over her shoulder at the street.

"You'll have to cross that one street, and there's no stop sign or light."

"But it's a residential neighborhood, which means less traffic."

"True." He nodded. "It can be done, though they need to put a stop sign there."

"You can go the other way around. It's longer, about twice as long but there is a crosswalk."

"I'll be okay. I can hear a car coming and I'll be using my cane. Now, let's take a look at the schedule. We're going shopping."

"Groceries?"

"No. I want to buy you something to put next to your other keepsakes; something that reminds you of me. Are you up for that?"

Wow. "Yeah. Thank you, honey." She read to him the times for the pickups and they decided to head back to his neighborhood where there were so many interesting little shops to explore. The bus picked them up a few moments later and Lee paid for the both of them before she could even put her hand into her bag.

The bus began moving before he was seated but he didn't even stumble. He sat down next to her and placed his hand lightly on her knee. "Home sweet home," he whispered playfully.

Back in Lee's eclectic little neighborhood, Tory led them to a second hand shop. Some people didn't like them, but she found great fines among the items that others had discarded as useless. Lee put away his cane and allowed her to loop her hands around his arm and to be his guide. She was pleased that he trusted her enough to do that, so she was very careful.

She loved watching him run his fingers along items, and the look of concentration on his face as he formed an image of it in his head. He looked like an inquisitive little kid and she realized that this is something that he probably loved doing but maybe hadn't had anyone to share with, either. Her heart opened up just a teeny bit more than it had previously.

After that shop, they went to a bookstore, but it was by his insistence not hers. "Wait." They paused just inside of the door and he pulled out his cane. He tapped the floor several times in different directions. He looked at her. "I can tell where things are by doing that."

"How?"

"The sound it gives off lets me know how close I am to things."

"If I let you go will you bump into something?"

"No. Let me go and I'll show you." She stepped back and he used his cane to test a tight circumference around himself as he moved forward. A group of people had stopped to talk and as he went around them they moved out of his way. A greeter came up to him.

"How are you today, sir? Can I help you find anything?"

"Books on tape please." The clerk offered her arm and Lee took it lightly.

"Sure, follow me. Was there something that you were looking for specifically?"

Lee followed, holding his cane perpendicular to his body as he the young woman guided him. She gave him an appreciative look as she led him to the display where the books on tapes were located. Tory came up behind them.

"Hi honey."

"Hi babe." He responded and held out his arm for her.

The sales woman pouted but pointed out some of the more popular recordings.

"I can take it from here." Tory replied, and the woman left reluctantly.

"There are a lot of displays and you didn't run into any of them. I guess you don't need me around." His cell phone rang before he could reply. He gave her a quick squeeze and retrieved it from his pocket. "Yep? Hi Mace. No, Tory and I are out together."

Macey--his sister. Tory picked up a tape and pretended to be interested in it and not listening to his conversation. She suspected that Roz had probably run to them complaining about the slutty fat girl with the dirty apartment. Tory's face burned.

Lee moved the phone from his mouth. "My sister says hi."

She smiled. "Oh, tell her I said hi."

"She wants us to come by for dinner, is that cool?"

"At the restaurant? Sure, that's fine."

"No, not at the restaurant, at her place. She's not working tonight."

"Oh, okay. Yeah that sounds good." She wasn't always comfortable in situations like dinner with people she didn't know well. And what if Roz showed up? What if Macey was just checking her out, like this was a big test that she might pass or fail? But she liked Macey just from their brief acquaintance so she focused on that.

"Okay, Mace. We'll be there. Yeah, that's fine. *Até logo*." After returning the phone to his pocket he took her hand and smiled warmly. "My brothers and sisters are good people. You'll like them."

"All of them?" She croaked.

"Yes. All of my brothers and sisters will be there and don't sound so nervous, *querida*--Roz will not be present." Oh Roz she could handle. That woman was just a secondary fixture in his life. But if his family didn't like her, now that was a whole other story.

CHAPTER 8

Tory felt distracted as they moved from shop to shop. They stopped for coffee and Tory still hadn't found anything that reminded her of Lee.

"It doesn't have to be today. We'll find something to put on your mantle."

"You want to be on my mantle?" She joked.

He reached out and took her hand. "I'd like to be among the things that you find precious." Tory moved her fingers, intertwining them with his.

"You already are," she whispered.

He kissed her fingers lightly and his rough growth of stubble tickled the back of her fingers. He had neglected his morning shave and the result was a rugged sexy look that kept her eyes glued to his face. She reached out and rubbed his cheek.

"So..." He said. "Are you getting tired of shopping? We can go back to my place and relax until dinner...?""Relax. Okay, I like to relax," she said breathlessly.

He retrieved his cell phone. "We're going to take a cab this time."

While they rode the short distance to his place, Tory leaned in and whispered to him.

"This is the most fun that I've ever had."

He nodded and leaned in. "For me, it's a toss-up between today and last night." She peeked at the cab driver and then quickly kissed him which caused him to laugh. Back at the apartment the two walked arm in arm into the building. Cat sauntered up to them, meowing loudly.

"Awww." Lee reached down and rubbed the tabby. "Did I forget to feed you? You didn't leave a gift in my bed did you?" He moved in a relaxed manner to the kitchen. "Honey, put on some music.

"She gave the stereo a wary look. "Oh...ok." It was the type of entertainment center that looked futuristic to her. She had a turntable that still sounded great despite the fact that it had seen its hay day back in the seventies. She found a remote control and hit the power button. Immediately the system came to life, lighting up like a space ship, but no music. She pressed the button for CD/DVD 1. Immediately loud Latin music came over the speakers and Tory almost jumped out of her skin. After a few moments she found the volume button and turned it down to something less ear shattering.

"Sorry!" He called from the kitchen. "I was practicing my dance moves before the date." She tried to imagine him dancing here all by himself. It was a sexy image. He returned to the living room carrying two glasses of wine and she met him halfway. She took the glass but before she could drink he pulled her to him.

"I've wanted to do this all morning," he leaned down and kissed her twice. The first kiss was light and gentle. The second kiss was deep and passionate; a sharing of tongues and the sucking of lips. She pulled back suddenly.

"What time do we meet your family for dinner?"

His hand rested on her rounded hip, fingers lightly stroking her there.

He sighed. "Actually, we can go over as early as we want but they'll be sitting down to eat at six." She knew that it was probably just after three o'clock now...

"How far away is it?"

"Walking distance. We could be there in fifteen minutes."

"So...we could leave here at five and be there at a decent time?"

His hands seemed to be having a fine time exploring her rear. "Is there anything in particular that you had a mind to do before dinner?"

She hid a grin and tried to sound serious. "Remember those sounds I made last night? Well, I was of a mind to make them again..."

Lee closed his eyes. "*Oh meu it dues*...Do you know what you do to me when you talk like that?" She trailed a finger down his toned belly, over the

111

button of his pants and then further over the slight bulge of his crotch. She felt him shudder. She was beginning to have an idea.

"Mmmm." He sighed in pleasure. "You should use your fingers to see me...an experiment. Are you game?"

"Close my eyes and see you by touch only?" But she really liked looking at him with eyes...of course, running her fingers over every line of his body wouldn't be too bad either. "I'm game!" They quickly finished their wine and then Lee took the glasses and whisked them away to the kitchen. In the bedroom she quickly stripped out of her clothes, taking care to drape them neatly over the chair since she'd be wearing them to meet his family.

Lee was less careful and he was naked in less than thirty seconds. He climbed into bed and lay with one arm folded behind his head. She forgot to breathe as she looked at this gorgeous naked man, already semi-erect because he wanted her. Her.

She walked to the bed naked and didn't remember for a second that she was once ashamed of her body for at the present moment all she could think of was how beautiful he made her feel. Once she was on the bed she did as she had indicated and closed her eyes. He reached up once and ran his fingers lightly over them just to check.

For a moment she just concentrated on the feel of his fingers as they left a trail down her neck, over her collarbone and then innocently between her breast. She didn't realize that she had been holding her breath until his fingers fell away and she found that she was slightly lightheaded.

Without opening her eyes she started her exploration at the top of his head where his light brown curls began. She ran her fingers through his short hair, rubbing the strands between her fingers as he had done to her days before. She allowed her nails to lightly graze his scalp and he groaned softly. Her fingers traced his brow, memorizing the shape of his face and then the slope of his nose and the curve of his lip. She felt compelled to bend down and kiss him then, and his lips were already to meet hers.

Before it could become too heated she sat up again, eyes still closed and concentrated on the feel of his neck. She knew instantly that he was ticklish there even though he didn't laugh out loud, but just by the way he flinched. She chuckled and moved away from the danger zone of his neck and to the light covering of hair on his sculptured chest. She loved the way her hands moved over the defined plains of his pecs. Her fingers flicked his nipples and his breath came out in a rush and she felt that his body was moving. Mmmm, she wanted to kiss him again, so this time she placed her lips on his nipple. She wanted to bite him and so she did, very gently. He groaned loudly and began moving again.

He evidently liked teeth being used on him so she trailed kisses over his chest while randomly gathering his flesh between her teeth. Each time she did this he sucked in a sharp breath and now she could tell that the movements he was making was the gyration of his hips. She placed her hand on his upper thigh where it met his pelvis and he moved his hips off the bed slightly, as if he was reaching up seeking her hands, but she kept them in the relative safe position on his thigh and pelvis.

She enjoyed this game. She wanted to run her fingers along his cock and she knew that he wanted it as well, but it would mark the end of the exploration and she wasn't ready to do that. She moved her hand up to his belly and dipped a finger into the well of his belly button.

"Ah..." He cried out and jumped. God, his skin was super sensitive. She leaned forward and used her tongue to explore his belly.

"Oh fuck...Tory..." His body began to gyrate. "I don't think I can take anymore." He growled and sat up, swiftly gripping her around her waist and pulling her down on top of him. "Ride me, *querida*." Without thought, her fingers wrapped around his shaft and he cried out. He was sensitive *and* vocal! She swung her leg over his body, straddling him while still lightly working his cock in her fist. He was breathing so hard that he was panting.

"Condom." She said. Her hips moved over his lap.

"Okay." He whispered but his hips continued to gyrate in rhythm with her, his breath coming out in soft grunts. "Yessss..." But he did not move to reach for a condom. "Oh baby, pleassse..." he begged suddenly. And this time she rubbed the head of his very swollen cock against her very swollen labia. She was so wet when she slipped herself over him. Was it this big last night? She was too tight, even as wet as she was, it would barely go inside.

Tory leaned forward, finding the right angle and though she was very tight he slowly entered her. He placed his hands on her full hips, holding her in place and then he rocked inside of her gently.

"Okay?"

"Yes." She said breathlessly. He increased his speed of his rocking hips and this time she was the one doing the groaning. Her body began to swirl, her head to spin as little electrical shocks began to jolt through her abdomen. Last night, she thought, had been the epitome of sex; but it was even better today! Today her body seemed to know how to respond and her vagina seemed to understand its purpose.

Her heart began to race and she felt almost over-whelmed by the convergence of sensations and emotions. Her mouth opened and she had to express herself in the only way that she knew how.

"Oh!" She cried out. "Ohhh, Lee. I love you Lee! Oh, I love you!"

He thrust into her faster. "Say it again, Tory!"

She squeezed her eyes closed and threw back her head. "I love you!"

He groaned even louder. "*Eu amo-te!* I love you, Tory!" And then he roughly pushed her off his lap and he grabbed his cock and abruptly ejaculated amidst soft groans. She watched him working himself to orgasm and found a decadent, voyeuristic pleasure in it. She knew that she would replay this moment for years within her fantasies.

"Oh, honey..." He panted an instant before drawing her back into his arms. He cradled her in one arm and with his free hand, slipped his fingers between the swollen, wet folds of her pussy. She sucked in a sharp breath and arched her back. He fingered her clit until she felt herself spiraling upward again. He moved his fingers away long enough to grip her hand and move it to replace his.

"Touch yourself." He commanded. She bit her lip and did as he asked. She felt his larger hand cover hers and he 'watched' with his hands as she rubbed and teased herself.

"Oh God, Tory...." He leaned forward, seeking out her nipple, sucking it roughly into his mouth, drawing on it until her legs began to shake and an orgasm slammed into her. She came yelling and crying out nonsense words until there was nothing more. She was spent. Distantly she was amazed that she had actually masturbated with a man. But not just a man; *her* man. And then she remembered crying out her love for him. For some reason that was more embarrassing than the mutual masturbation. But he had said it too and that thought brought a smile on her face.

He placed his head along side of hers. "That was amazing."

"It was. It gets better and better."

He chuckled. "Indeed. When you're with someone you love, then the feeling is extraordinary." He pulled her into his arms again and held her against him. "Thank you, *querida*. I love you and I am so happy that I found you. You make me feel more alive than anyone else ever has."

She placed her lips against his. "I love you." She said softly while kissing him repeatedly.

His tongue ran across her lips. "I love you." He murmured.

"Tu amo..." She experimented with the foreign words.

117

"*Eu te amo*," he corrected. "I love you." He continued to kiss her gently.

"*Eu te amo*, Lee."

"*Eu amo-te Tory. Estou tão feliz. Quero-te oura vez...*"

She pulled back. "What?"

"I love you, Tory. I'm so very happy. I want you again."

Sure enough, when she reached between them he was already rising. She smiled. There could not be a luckier woman in the world.

They made love once more, slowly, luxuriating in the feel of each other and this time they did not forgo the condom so when Lee again came, he was able to bring her to climax along with him. After, they showered and redressed. It wasn't quite five but she was anxious to get dinner over with.

Tory knew that she shouldn't look at it this way but she'd never had to meet a boyfriend's relatives before. It spoke volumes for Lee that he wanted her there with him. He could have sent her home. They walked down the street hand in hand and though he said that she was his cane, she knew that he was the real guide here.

They reached a brownstone building. Several little kids that had been playing on the stoop ran up to them.

"Hi Uncle Lee!" They crashed in to him, from the youngest that looked no older than three to the eldest that was as tall as Tory. He seemed to be prepared for the tackle and accommodated each of them with hugs. She even got a hug from the three year old and that put a happy smile on her face. The children were gorgeous, some pudgy, some stick thin and all happy to see their Uncle.

"Hey guys, don't knock over my girlfriend."

"Sorry, Ma'am." One of the smaller ones said solemnly while watching her with big light brown eyes.

"I don't mind being bowled over, as long as it's with hugs and kisses." She hadn't realized that it was an invitation but suddenly she was swarmed by little bodies as well. Lee laughed merrily and rescued her by picking up two of the smallest ones who giggled happily.

Someone darted up the stairs of the building and Tory could hear the distant voice shouting that Lee was here with a girl. Her stomach did a nervous flip. Adults would be converging on them soon. Lee took her hand again and led them carefully up the stairs. He seemed to know how to expertly maneuver between darting little bodies, perspective toys as well as managing the stairs without a cane.

Tory checked out the pretty building as they headed up a flight of stairs. "This is your sister Macey's home?"

"Actually this building is owned by my brother. Four families live here. Macey and Senna live on the top floor. My brother Paulo, who owns the building, has one of the first floor units. And...two other families occupy the other units." Intuitively she knew that one of those families was Roz's, so she didn't even bother to ask.

"They wanted me to live here but...it was too much like living at home. My family is very close knit and there just wouldn't be any real privacy if I lived here." The door to the upstairs apartment opened before they reached it and a blond woman came out to greet them.

"Lee! There you are. *Anda cá*." She gripped Tory's hand. "Tory? Nice to meet you, hon. My name is Kaye, I'm Paulo's wife." She pulled them inside and the apartment was swarming with bodies. Swarming might be an overstatement, the apartment was thankfully huge, and it was filled with people. She began to panic at the idea of having to remember these names.

"Dinner smells good, Kaye." He turned to Tory. "Kaye is like a sister to me. She and Paulo have always been together even back on Flores. Any picture I have of Paulo is with Kaye not too far behind."

"Ah, indeed, I was your first babysitter."

Another woman stepped through the gathering of bodies that came to greet them. "You?

I remember it was me that was changing that boy's diapers."

Lee reached out to the woman with a happy smile. "Tory, this is my oldest sister, Francie. She is like a second mother to me." The two hugged lovingly.

"I've had to paddle you like I was your Mama on several occasions, too." She chuckled. Then she gave Tory a huge smile.

"Tory, nice to meet you." She pulled Tory into a hug, which surprised her, and then other people came forward to greet and hug Lee and she always received a hug right along with him. There were brothers and sisters and then their spouses and the introductions seemed to go on forever. The kids ignored them as they went running in and out of the apartment. She had a distant idea that one day she might have little caramel colored children that would be running about right along with them, getting yelled at good-naturedly when they bumped into something or slammed the door. It brought a pleased smile to her face. It was much too early to be having those thoughts, but her mind couldn't stop it.

Macey squeezed her hand drawing her attention back around. "Nice seeing you out of the restaurant."

"Thanks for inviting me."

"Inviting you? You are family. You must always come!" She grabbed her arm and led her away. Tory gave Lee a quick backward look. He was talking to a man named Rafael and he called out jokingly, "Take care of my woman, Mace!"

"*Pára quieto*," the young woman waved away his words. "Come on. I'll get you something to drink." They went into a pretty kitchen. It was big and delicious aromas were coming from it. Tory was suddenly starving. The room had a homey feel despite the fact that it had commercial size appliances. Yes, this would be the kitchen of a restaurant owner and a member of an extra large family. But it also had a relaxed and comfortable appearance. Pictures of family and drawings by kids decorated the refrigerator or a bulletin board. There were all kinds of canisters and jars filled with spices and pickled items. It was just the type of place that she would love to explore.

Kaye was there tending to a huge roasted meat; leg of lamb? And another wife was slicing cucumbers. It looked like she was making a salad. She gave Tory a warm smile. Macey moved to the refrigerator.

"What would you like to drink? I made a rum punch."

"That sounds good, thanks."

Kaye hefted the meat and placed it back into the oven. "I'm happy you said what you did to

Roz." Kaye dusted off her fingers and then placed her hands on her more than ample hips. She was big enough that she was more than plump, but from the expert application of her make-up, to her pretty blond hair and the way she carried herself, this woman was very pretty.

Macey placed the cold rum drink into Tory's hand, nodding in agreement. "Don't get us wrong. Roz is family, but you are my brother's woman and that means she got trumped." Tory hid a smile.

"Yes." The third woman in the room said. "You don't make a play for a woman's man right in her face!"

"Yes, but Roz always thought that she was the boss over Lee." Kaye added. She was slicing thick crusty bread. "We love Roz and we don't spend a lot of time gossiping about family."

Macey took a sip of her own rum drink. "But we're telling you this; that *maluca*, was wrong."

Francie entered the room; the eldest, along with another sister, also as plump and shapely as the others. Her name was Senna.

Senna was nodding even though she had entered at the tail end of the conversation. "Don't worry about Roz. She told Leticia about the fight; she and Leticia are best friends, but even Leticia had to say, Girl, *apanhada do juízo*?! You are married to Brice and have two kids!' She said, 'Give that girl a chance. She will make my brother happy.'" Senna nodded her head as if that was a given fact.

Francie began placing the sliced bread into a pretty woven basket lined with a linen napkin. "Well I will guarantee that Roz thought we'd all be on her side." She gave Tory a steady look. "But I know that Lee has been very lonely. If she cared about that she would have left her husband long ago and approached him correctly. *"Não te parece?"* And it was as if she was asking for her agreement.

"I...yes." Tory nodded and she did agree. Obviously Roz had been harboring those feelings for years.

Senna poured herself some rum punch. "I knew she liked him." She said knowingly.

"Well I didn't," Francie announced while placing the baking sheet into the oven. "If I had known that she had scandalous ideas I would have told her about herself. Tory, hand me the butter from the refrigerator, please."

Tory liked listening to the women talking even if she hadn't added more than two words to the conversation. They didn't make her feel self-conscious. She passed the woman an industrial sized tub of butter.

A tall dark haired man entered the room. She remembered that he was Paulo; Kaye's husband. He looked to be in his forties and had strands of grey in his curly hair. His skin tone was much darker then Lee's and his eyes were hazel. He was really gorgeous even with a pouch for a belly and about fifty extra pounds on his tall frame.

"What are you hens talking about?" He gave Tory a friendly wink while everyone else chastised and berated him both in English and Portuguese until he grabbed several beers from the fridge and slipped back out of the kitchen.

"Tory, come over here and give me a hand," a woman said. She was several years older than her and Tory had no hope of remembering what her name was as she was not a sibling of Lee's, but married to one of his brothers; Rafael or Carlo, she didn't remember which. "I'm going to show you how to make the *aletria*, eh?"

"I'd love to. Let me wash my hands." She went to the sink and quickly washed while the women chatted and described the dishes that they'd have. The woman poured milk into a large pot to boil. It was nearly the entire gallon of milk, but then again it was a very large family. She instructed her to pour a cup and a half of sugar into the simmering liquid along with a couple of teaspoons of salt while the woman went about cracking a dozen eggs and beating them up quickly along with more sugar.

"Ladle some of the boiling milk into the eggs...that's it. Good." The woman beat them for a bit longer and then set the egg mixture aside. She then grabbed a box of vermicelli noodles. "Back home we made this with rice but here we make it with noodles." The two of them broke the hard noodles into the boiling milk and sugar concoction. Once that was done and the noodles were cooked in the boiling milk, they took it off the heat.

Kaye removed the leg of lamb from the oven to rest in the pan and Tory poured the tempered eggs mixture into the pot of vermicelli and milk until it made a beautiful custard. She smiled in pleasure once it was poured into a shallow glass dish. She was instructed to sprinkle cinnamon across the top and it was placed in the refrigerator to cool. She had prepared her first Portuguese dish!

"Dinner will be ready in a few minutes." Kaye shooed her out of the kitchen even though she had been having a good time cooking with the women. Of course, being kicked out of the kitchen and back to Lee wasn't a bad deal either. Senna placed a beer in her hands.

"Give that to Lee, he's probably due for his next one."

"Ok." Before she was completely out the kitchen door Macey placed a hand on her shoulder. "Welcome to the family. We are all kind of crazy and we're loud at times and talk too much but we kiss a lot too and hug and are loyal to the end. Whenever you're around any of us, you have allies. Do you understand?"

She was so touched that her eyes stung. If this was Azorean hospitality then she was blessed. She looked at each of the women in the room and knew that the sentiment was shared by all.

"Thank you for making me feel so welcome. I truly understand why Lee is such a special man, it runs in the family." She went to the living room but didn't see Lee or the other men, just some of the kids still racing about.

"Where is your Uncle Lee?" She asked one of the children.

"In the family room watching soccer." The child pointed out a connecting room and she peeked inside to the sight of several men and some of the older children watching a big screen television. It was apparently set to an international channel and a soccer match was broadcasting, the announcer speaking rapidly in a foreign language. Suddenly several of the men jumped up and cheered, among them was Lee. He was listening intently.

"Uncle Lee, Tory is here." A boy about sixteen said. Lee turned in his seat and held out his hand from where he was sitting on the couch.

"Hey, *querida*. Welcome back." Paulo stood and moved to the chair, allowing her room to sit next to Lee. She smiled her thanks to him. Lee pulled Tory into his arms snuggling with her and she passed him the beer.

"*Cerveja* for you, honey." She said.

"Where's my wife with my *cerveja*?" Paulo asked playfully.

"Last I checked she was carving the biggest leg of lamb ever known to man."

Rafael winked at her. They were a playful, winking family. "We're going to have to trade our wives in for new ones like you, Tory."

"I heard that!" The woman that had taught her to make the *aletria* was suddenly in the doorway holding several beers. "For that I take these right back to the kitchen-"

There were several protests and she pretended to relent, and walked around the room passing out the beers to the adults, slapping the hand of the 16 year old when he reached out for one, until she finally ended by sitting in the lap of her husband, presenting him with a kiss and the last beer.

"Do you like soccer, Tory?" Lee asked.

"I've never watched it."

Everyone in the room got quiet and stared at her as if she had just announced that she'd flown in from the moon.

"Some American's don't watch soccer." The sixteen year old said. "They watch American football." Someone scowled. "American football has too much standing around and not enough action."

"I've seen bits and pieces of soccer matches; on the news. I saw a soccer player kick some guy in the head." Tory said. His scalp had split and blood had poured from it like a fountain. She'd also seen fans chase down a referee and give him a beat down. It seemed a bit violent to her.

Everyone rushed in a once to try to explain the game to her. She was too embarrassed to admit that she had no idea what they were talking about.

"Which team are we rooting for?" She asked.

"Portugal's team is a Selecção." She watched intently, people moving quickly back and forth after a little ball. Damn, men around the world weren't all that different; excited over this. But soon Kaye entered the room and ushered the kids to come eat. And then a few minutes later the rest of the family was seated.

Two card tables had been set up for the kids and the once smaller dining room table had the extenders in place so that it was now twice as big. The food was set up buffet style on the hutch and therefore there were no place settings present, just several glasses; water and wine. Tory and Lee stood in line for the food and Lee said something in Portuguese. Several of the women responded likewise. Lee turned to her.

"Nothing too adventurous today on the menu. We'll have to persuade them that you can hang with the rest of us Azoreans."

Her eyes scanned the feast before them. "I'm not complaining. Everything looks mouth watering." She passed him a plate and he told her everything that he wanted and she loaded him up. There was the roasted lamb, rice, and fat slices of a bread called *pão de milho* which literally translated to corn bread, although it was nothing like American cornbread.

"In the Azores, it is much easier to grow corn so traditionally our bread is made with corn flour instead of wheat and yeast instead of baking powder," he explained.

"Well…" Macey interjected. "We have *broa* that is wheat based but mainly when we are eating soups and stews." Tory tried not to look confused. She made sure to take a slice of both types of bread.

In addition to the bread were several different vegetable dishes as well as a familiar dish made with beans and rice. There was a cheese plate, a huge platter of the little neck clams just like the ones that she was served at the restaurant, a cucumber and tomato salad drizzled with vinegar and oil dressing, and lastly, her *aletria*. They were led to their seats and before they began to eat Paulo stood and held up a wine glass.

"Cheers to our guest; our new friend, Tory. We all hope that you will join us for many more such family dinners…and feel free to invite us to your place, otherwise we are known to show up and throw impromptu parties." Everyone chuckled.

Counting the children there were easily twenty-five people in the apartment. Her small home wouldn't hold half this.

"You're all welcome anytime." She said honestly.

Lee shushed her. "They will take you seriously, love. We withdraw that invitation." He said playfully. Tory fell in love with Lee's family during dinner as they all rushed to talk and to be heard but with love. She drank, she ate, she laughed and she was doing it beside the man of her dreams. Again she had to wonder, could any woman be luckier?

CHAPTER 9

They walked home even though eight different people offered to drive them. By the time they finished saying their goodbyes and assuring everyone that they wanted to stretch their legs and walk, it was almost ten pm. They'd eaten her delicious desert and Lee promised that it was the best *aletria* he'd ever had.

As they walked out of the building Tory caught the movement of a curtain and she saw Roz there looking out at them. Her expression was impassive, and Tory didn't retreat from the look. Had it really been this morning that she'd almost made the biggest mistake of her life and allowed Roz to run her away from Lee's home? How stupid she'd almost been. Maybe there was more to Roz than what she'd shown to Tory. She knew that there would come a time when the two of them would be in the same location but she also knew that there would never come a time when she'd ever forget that Roz wanted Lee and was rejected by him. She squeezed his arm, which was hooked through hers and he turned to her and smiled.

"I told you, you'd like them. My family is good people."

"They are awesome people."

He sighed. "I don't want you to go home. How long can you stay?"

"Until tomorrow." Then she had to prepare for work for the coming week and she wanted to give her home a really good cleaning. That comment Roz had made really haunted her.

He grinned. "I have one more night with you."

She felt her body begin to react to his words. "I hope there will be more to come." He nodded in agreement.

Back at his loft, she was beginning to feel at home. She slipped off her shoes and placed them safely in the corner, then she greeted Cat with a scratch behind her/his ears; she wasn't sure what sex the animal was.

Lee turned on the sound system again and found Reggaeton for them to listen to. She was a little tired, but the memory of their night at the club overpowered the need to sit down and relax.

"Come here, Tory. I want to show you something." She placed her hands in his and his body began to sway sensually to the music. She watched him for a moment until she was able to mimic his simple repetitive steps. Still holding his hand she moved from side to side, hips swaying to the beat. He moved in closer until their bodies moved as one.

"*Bom.*" He said pleased. "*Muito bom.*" Then his hips began to move rapidly and she hesitated, still swaying as he originally had been. She would never be able to do that in a million years.

"Just wiggle your hips." She tried and it looked more like a shudder. "Imagine..." His fingers began to creep down her spine. "...a caterpillar has fallen down the back of your shirt and you have to wiggle it out." And then she suddenly knew the movement she'd need in order to do that, and her hips began wiggling. Tory laughed out loud. She felt like Shakira! His hands moved to her hips.

"*Bom!* Ooo damn, baby. That is sexy and you are such a fast learner." He took a step back from her. "Watch me." He began with his basic body-swaying move and then he came forward and then backward rapidly. "Cha cha cha step, you've seen before, no?"

"Cha cha. I can do that." She did. She did know how to do the electric slide.

"Mambo?" And then he did a quick mambo step.

"Oh...kay." She tried it and it didn't look anything like what he'd done. He kept doing it, very very slowly, over and over. Finally she was doing a mambo. She giggled happily. He took her hand and together they made different combinations of the mambo, cha cha and the hip swaying and hip shaking.

"There baby. Now you know how to dance Reggaeton. And you're good at it. You're not afraid to move those beautiful hips." She looked back at her ass as if it were a separate attachment.

"These hips sometimes have a life of their own; they move even when I don't want them to."

He kissed her sensually. "They can move for me as often as they like. I love your hips." His hands held her there as his kisses trailed down her neck. "I love this neck and these ears...and of course these breasts."

The couple moved to the bedroom and Tory learned that there was a reason that the doggy style was one of the most popular sexual positions. Afterwards, they lay in the spoon position and Tory murmured to him.

"I don't see how it's possible but today was even more fun than yesterday."

"Mmm." He placed a light kiss on the back of her neck. "I agree. She felt him prop himself up on his elbow. "Tory?"

"Hmm?"

He hesitated. "Yesterday you mentioned that you weren't a virgin. I...got the distinct impression that the loss of your virginity was against your will." She turned in bed to face him. "If I'm being too nosey then please forgiv-"

She placed her finger on his lips.

"It's okay." This was something she had never shared with anyone other than her parents and only because they had a need to know. "I went to college to be a pharmacist." She grimaced. "I can't even imagine why I wanted to be a pharmacist now...it seems like so long ago." She sighed.

"I was kind of outgoing back then. I used to go to parties and drink too much with my friends. But I wasn't..." She cleared her throat trying not to allow her voice to shake so. "I wasn't a fast girl, I was just an eighteen year old girl that had left home for the first time. My friends and I went to a bar and I wasn't all that drunk. But I met a guy. He didn't go to my University and he was a little older. He seemed kinda cool and I...well I told him I'd go to another club with him." Her breath was coming faster and she didn't like that after so many years, thinking about that night still did that.

"I...we never got to the club. He pulled down a dead end street and he raped me. I suppose that there are a lot of things that I could have done had I not been drunk-"

"Tory."

She stopped talking and looked up, trying to read his tight expression. "Yes?"

"It wasn't your fault."

"I got into a car with a guy I didn't know..."

"*Bela*, you are so sweet and trusting. Those are two qualities that you never lost." He sighed and his voice grew tight. "What happened to that guy?"

"Nothing. The cops never found him and I dropped out of school because I was simply too scared to stay there."

His brow knit. "The guy that did that to you is still out on the streets?"

She nodded. "I believe so."

He gripped her hand and pulled it to his lips. He kissed her fingers lightly. "I'm so sorry. I wish that there was something that I could do-"

"You already have, honey. Just me feeling loved by you-"

"No. I mean, I wish that I could kill him for you."

She was silent for a moment. "I have killed him a million times in my head."

He paused. "How? Tell me how you've killed him."

Slowly she described the slow torture and castration of her attacker. Lee listened intently, nodding his full acceptance of her punishment and at times adding his own descriptions where hers were lacking. Somehow, after doing that she felt almost good. He pulled her into his arms and held her against his chest, and she slept listening to the beating of his heart.

The next day she could have lingered but she got up, dressed and after kissing and hugging Lee goodbye, Tory went to the bus stop so that she could go home. That evening after she'd finished cleaning her apartment and doing the laundry her phone rang and it was Lee explaining how much he missed her. He'd gone to the grocers with one of his sisters and had gotten his shopping done and now he was thinking about her dancing.

"Oh. I got you a present. I'll give it to you tomorrow on the bus." He said.

"A present? You found something for the mantle?"

"No. This present you aren't going to want to keep on the mantle...maybe a little closer to your person."

"So...are you going to give it to me on the bus?"

He sighed. "Tory, you know what you do to me when you talk dirty...But if I could give IT to you on the bus, I most certainly would. But the present I have for you — now that I can manage on the bus."

They talked for almost an hour and then she showered and put on pajama bottoms and a tee shirt. She tugged at the loose waistband and then at the seat of the pants. They were usually so

138

tight...Tory went to the restroom and stepped on the scale.

Oh my God...she'd lost nine pounds. She'd lost nine pounds in less than a week! It had once taken her three months to lose nine pounds, and she'd just now done it in five days! She squealed and jumped up and down. Walking, dancing...making love, not to mention eating lighter; of course she would lose weight! She gripped her butt. She didn't want to lose too much, though. Her man liked her with some substance.

The next morning she took special care in her appearance, wearing a nice pantsuit and blouse as well as running shoes. Her heels she tucked into a briefcase along with a peanut butter and jelly sandwich that she'd thrown together for her lunch. And then right when she thought that the bus would be nearing its destination she took off sprinting down the street. Sure enough the thing was speeding to the stop, just as she was. If she didn't get there first it would just keep going even though the bus driver would clearly see her running for it.

Her hands pumped as she sprinted and she beat the bus! When the doors opened she was panting and sweating, but she had her change tucked securely in her suit jacket. She climbed up the stairs triumphantly and smirked at the bus driver. Lee was sitting in his usual seat and his back straightened and his eyes widened. He held out his hand palm up and she placed the change in it, then she sat down in the empty seat next to his while he fed her change in for her.

When he sat back down he had two bright red spots on his cheek. She leaned in towards him and whispered.

"Hi honey, what's wrong?"

"Your breathing...that's the sound! It is the sound you make when you've been made love to very thoroughly..." he whispered back. Tory swallowed back her giggles. It was the effect she had been going for.

The other commuters on the bus watched them curiously and maybe in some cases, incredulously as the two lovers whispered back and forth, chuckling and holding hands. Lee reached into his pocket and pulled out an object and handed it to her.

It was a key. She gave him a quick look.

"I had it made yesterday. I want you to feel free to come by whenever you want, *queridu*." Despite the other commuters she leaned forward and kissed him lightly. Someone made a low wolf whistle and others giggled. Yikes, she hadn't intended to put on a show. He reached for his duffel bag and pulled the rope to indicate his stop.

"May I come over and visit you tonight?"

"Yes," she grinned.

"Okay, see you after work. *Adeus, bela.*"

"*Adeus!*" He was suddenly gone and she already missed him.

After work she called him on his cell phone. She was quickly searching for something casual to wear. "I'm going to meet you at the bus stop."

He chuckled. "You won't need to do that."

"Well I just don't want you to get turned around or anything-"

"I can't get lost in a five minute walk from the bus stop to your apartment. Hold on." Tory heard her doorbell ring. "Honey, I have to hang up now, I'm at my girlfriend's house."

"What?!" She cried out happily. She sprinted to the front door and opened it and there he was looking sexy in Dockers and a crisp white button up shirt. She moved quickly into his arms and they spent a few moments kissing right there in the entrance.

"*Eu falto-o.*" She spoke in Portuguese; I miss you. "*Eu quero-o.*" I want you...

"How-?" He began in surprise.

"Babel fish." He laughed out loud. "I practiced all morning." He was very proud of her and didn't have the heart to tell her that the online translation was definitely not right. He just enjoyed the fact that she would try. Lee decided in that second that he would be in charge of her lessons and that before long she would be speaking Portuguese just like a native of the Azores.

She led him into the apartment.

"Honey, show me how to position the rooms so that it's easy for you to navigate."

He looked around. "Just don't change the position of the furniture without warning me. Even a few inches throws me off. Other than that, I'll learn the layout. He was carrying his duffel bag and he reached into one of the zipper portions.

"Oh, I found something for the mantle."

"Something to remind me of you?"

He nodded and withdrew his cane that was folded into a small bundle.

"Your cane? You're going to still need this..."

"My old cane. They get bent or the tip comes off. I haven't used this one in years." She took it and smiled. She unfolded it and ran her fingers down the sections.

"Baby...this is PERFECT! I love it!" She placed it on the mantle next to the tarnished bell and it fit wonderfully. "Come see it." He moved forward carefully and reached out with a light touch, his fingers moving over the items until they stopped at the cane.

"It looks good here."

CHAPTER 10
3 MONTHS LATER

She felt a gentle tug on her nipple, the warm flick of a tongue and then the sound of soft sighs. Tory's eyes remained closed as she snuggled closer to Lee, her legs going around his lower body, capturing him between her thick thighs.

He struggled, not to get away, but to seek her warm inviting core. While continuing to lap at her breast, he thrust forward, slipping into her yielding opening and hearing her gasp of pleasure. She always wondered how one could be so hard so early in the morning. Lee was like steel encased in velvet. He pumped his hips, slipping that magnificent piece of manhood into her only to withdraw it and push it into her again—so many times that she was lightheaded with need. She cried out words that had no meaning and yet he understood each command, every plea, and every moan of pleasure.

Later, the couple lay cuddled in each other's arms. "Good morning, *bela*." He pulled Tory into his arms tighter, nuzzling her neck.

She placed her lips against the soft curls of his head. "'Morning." With a sigh she pulled herself out of his arms. "You shower, I'll start the coffee."

His lips curled into a playful pout. "Oh? We can't shower together?"

"No," She said firmly, "or we'll never get to work on time." She hurried to the bathroom to pee, admiring Lee's perfect physique as he trailed in after her and turned on the shower. Once upon a time, Tory would have been too embarrassed to use the toilet with anyone else in the room. But Lee thought her modesty was silly considering their level of intimacy. He also had to remind her that he couldn't see what she was doing on the toilet anyways. She quickly flushed and washed her hands and he glanced at her over his shoulder.

"You sure, *querida*?" He was holding back the shower curtain and looking towards her expectantly. Mmm mmm mmm, she thought. His unruly hair was tousled about his head and his morning stubble made him look rugged. The muscles in his toned body stood out like he worked out every single day even though he didn't. Her eyes lingered on his heavy manhood. Damn...

Okay," she relented. She was addicted to him. Sometimes she felt as if she had to grab as much joy from him as she could because somehow she would be awakened from this wonderful dream and she wanted as many memories of him that she could gather. He held out his hand to her and she took it as she joined him in the shower. He positioned her in front of the spray and stood behind her, his hands traveling over her front, helping the water to wet her. He picked up a sponge and applied her body wash and then proceeded to wash her thoroughly. His hand trailed over each curve, each fold and each dimple of her larger than average body.

For a moment she held her breath and tensed before remembering that she had no need to be ashamed. He found her weight to be a plus and not a negative. She watched him as he lovingly washed her body and knew that he didn't just accept her fat as 'something to be ignored or dealt with'. Lee liked her extra bits. She smiled and sighed. He urged her to turn so that he could wash her back, being careful not to get her hair wet. He had to be taught that black women did not wash their hair every single day and if it got wet then out came the blow dryer and the curling iron.

He turned her again and pressed against her back. She felt the sponge slipping between her thighs and then he was lathing her there, causing her body to tingle again. He was very thorough until she had to take the sponge from him with a giggle.

"Okay baby, I think it's clean now."

146

He blushed and grinned sheepishly. "I can't get enough of you Tory."

Her smile fell from her lips as she watched him. "Then I truly am the luckiest woman in the world." He shook his head slightly and she didn't understand what it meant but she applied his body wash and began to wash him in turn.

She took pleasure in noting that he was again erect, and it wasn't her fault that she was compelled to spend a great deal of time making sure *that* portion of his body was clean until he could take no more and cried out in release. She gripped him in her soapy fist and pumped her hand rapidly until she had worked every last drop from him. Lee slumped on his feet, panting.

"Now you-" His fingers slid along the crease between her thighs and she gripped his wrist with a gasp and stopped him.

"Baby, rain check?"

"Are you sure? I don't want you at work all day thinking that I'm a selfish bastard."

She grabbed the handheld shower and rinsed the last of the suds off their bodies. "I think about you all day every single day, and I promise that I've *never* thought anything remotely close to that about you." He was the most insatiable man, and she loved every second of the attention! There wasn't a day that went by that they didn't have sex in one form or another — even when it was time for her monthly cycle.

When she felt that they were sufficiently clean she leaned forward and kissed him. He pulled her possessively close and enjoyed her mouth before swatting her lightly on the ass.

"Okay, okay, enough. We are going to be late." She scowled and he chuckled. She wrapped her robe around herself and then hurried into the kitchen to start the coffee and to heat up the last of the tea ring that they had bought over the weekend.

While he shaved she went through the closet for one of the dresses she had brought over. In order to remain impromptu, she had a selection of clothes at his place and he had some at hers. It wasn't uncommon for either to spend days during the week at the others home, however because Cat still needed to be tended to it was generally his place that they ended up at. They hadn't slept apart in months. She found herself wondering if he would invite her to live with him. She would. She wouldn't hold out for a ring or anything.

This was the real world and she was an adult in an adult relationship. She didn't need the fairytale; she just needed to be in the NOW. Her mother had asked tentatively if she was living with him because she had called the apartment instead of her cell phone on several occasions…or perhaps her mother was just testing her—trying to catch her. Why did that thought make her blush? She was an adult and there was nothing wrong with having a sexual relationship with her boyfriend!

When she returned to the kitchen, Lee had already prepared her coffee just the way she liked it and was waiting for her so that they could enjoy their breakfast together. She paused and watched him move confidently to the cat kibble to fill Cat's bowl. He was blind but more graceful than a lot of people she knew; including herself.

"I'm going to go back to my place after work, babe," she said. He raised a brow at her. "I have to get more clothes."

"Okay, I'll pack a bag and swap out some clothes, too." They finished their coffee and tea ring and then left the loft apartment hand in hand, a backpack over his shoulders containing his fresh clothes and some of her dirty ones.

Once in the elevator, they took the familiar route to the subbasement parking area. Tory still couldn't stop the smile of joy that covered her face when she set eyes on the vehicle parked all alone in the large underground parking area. They had only been dating a few weeks when Lee had her take a look at some research that he was doing on the computer. He announced that he was going to buy a car. She remembered laughing but he was very serious.

"I can't drive, *querida*, but you can. You do have a driver's license, don't you?"

"I do...but-"

"Then it's settled. The choices are between these three and I need you to tell me which one you think looks best."

She had given him a strange look, not sure how to take the information. She couldn't tell him that he couldn't buy a car, and obviously she wouldn't tell him that she wouldn't drive him places...

She had looked at the computer and then her brow had shot up. "Uh...that's a Mercedes Benz."

"Ah, yes; the E-class. It has rear collision and side airbags, collision warning, night vision, and lane departure warning."

"Ok..." The next car was a Volvo and was very sporty. Lee announced that it had several alerts that he liked including a driver alert system that detected tired drivers. She giggled wondering if she would have to wear some type of monitor when driving it. The final car was an Audi A6. It was a tough decision but she told him that she preferred the look of the Volvo S60.

He had closed the lid on the laptop and said no more about it. The next day they took a cab to the dealership and then later they drove home in his brand new car. She knew that Lee wasn't hurting for money but she just didn't realize that he had it like that. She got the pleasure of selecting a beautiful caramel colored car with tan leather interior. It felt wrong but she couldn't deny that it had thrilled her at the same time.

Tory popped back to the present and watched Lee move to the back of the car. She popped open the trunk for him and then he stowed the backpack there and climbed into the passenger seat. No sooner did she have the car started before he was fiddling with the iPod player. She was suddenly hearing the relaxing sounds of Júlio Pereira's mandolin and she couldn't help but marvel at how much she had learned about the Portuguese and specifically the Azorean culture in these brief three months.

A short time later she dropped him off in front of his office and sat in the car watching him use his cane to tap out his location. Incredibly he moved directly to the entrance and disappeared into the building. Lee didn't understand just how amazing it was that he could find his way nearly as good as any sighted person. She sighed and then hurried off to her own office.

CHAPTER 11

"It's Monday. The Jewel is going to be serving seafood *cataplana* today," Lee said later that evening. *Cataplana* is what they called paella. Tory had intended to head straight back to the apartment. She was a little tired. Mondays were always rough because she hated leaving behind their lovefest weekends for the reality of the real world. Mmmm but the *cataplana* at the Jewel of the Azores was the best thing in the world. And it also meant that she wouldn't have to cook. Tory had gained a renewed love for cooking since being introduced to the das Torres family. Their lives revolved around food, which is the reason that even though she had dropped several pounds she was destined to remain a 'big girl.'

"Mmm that sounds good, baby. Let's do that." They had to search for parking. The Jewel had been featured in the city newspaper and now reservations were a must—well at least for anyone other than family. One of the nephews had designed a website and the traffic there was unbelievable. There was even talk of starting a second location. Tory couldn't be more proud of her 'sisters' accomplishments.

They walked quietly to the restaurant, holding hands. "Are you okay, honey?" he asked. She smiled and leaned her head against his broad shoulder as they walked.

"Yes, it's just optimistic Monday." They had donned a new phrase for Mondays so that they could keep in mind not to be too negative. Mondays didn't have to be viewed as the mark of impending Armageddon, it was just another day in the week. He placed his arm around her body and gave her a gentle squeeze.

"Honey, I know that you aren't happy with your job." She wanted to deny it but didn't. "Please think about going back to school."

"Yeah, but I don't know what career I want."

"Well, maybe you can just get a business degree, eh?"

She shrugged. "I guess I could make that work for me. I'll think about it." She didn't want to admit that she liked the little world that she existed in with Lee and his family. She just had no desire to change anything, not even to venture off to school and spend valuable time studying instead of making love and dancing and eating with her man. She had new best friends, a new boyfriend and a life that she loved. True she didn't like her job but she needed it to pay her bills and that was that.

They reached the restaurant and as usual, Rosalind was the hostess on duty. As normal the two women ignored each other and the couple moved to take seats at the bar. Tory was aware that Lee and Roz had begun speaking again but that was normally when she wasn't around. She'd asked him about it once but he dismissed it by saying that Roz knew not to say a word to her unless Tory was ready to approach her first. Thus far she had no desire to do that. Tory realized that just because Roz was a part of the lives of the others didn't mean that she had to be friends with the woman. Besides, it still smarted that she had deigned to call her home dirty. Roz had tried very hard to embarrass her in front of her man, and thankfully it had all back-fired on her.

"Hey you, two!" They turned to see Kaye and Paulo heading for them. Everyone hugged and before she knew it almost all of Lee's brothers, sisters, nieces and nephews were there hugging and kissing them. Wow, she knew the paella was good but, wow...

Macey grabbed her hand. "Come, we have a big table." She looked at Lee who didn't seem to think anything was strange about their 'family' table being used on a Monday. She couldn't remember an occasion when the family had ever held a gathering on a Monday. Lee and Tory were seated next to each other and then the wine began to flow. A cheese tray moved up and down the table along with other tapas trays. Francie joined them a short while later carrying a huge paella pan nearly overflowing and bubbling with spicy goodness.

Lee cleared his throat and tapped his wine glass with his desert spoon. "Before we dig into this delicious meal, I wanted to thank you all for coming together on a Monday. I know you all partied pretty hard over the weekend."

There were loud shouts of agreement and Tory found her brow knitting. What the…he called the gathering?

Lee turned to her and she could see him swallow past a lump in his throat. All of a sudden she understood and her eyes grew wide. Oh my God…

He took her hand in his and squeezed it gently. "Tory, since I've known you, I've been so very happy. I used to think that I knew what happiness was but I was completely clueless."

Tory thought she was going to have a heart attack. How was it possible that her heart could be beating so hard in her chest?! She stared at him with a shocked expression on her face; happy that he couldn't see it even if his family could.

"Tory, I love you. I want to live with you for the rest of my life. I want us to make a family together and have a houseful of brown and tan skinned children. I want to take care of you. And I want to marry you."

155

Her palms were soaking wet and she was shaking like a leaf. She snatched one of her hands from his to cover her mouth, eyes stinging as she rapidly nodded her head. The cheers went up around the table, as well as around the restaurant where the guests had apparently stopped what they were doing to listen to the proposal.

She noticed that even though everyone at the table had stood, Lee was still seated and watching her expectantly, unable to 'see' her response. She dropped her hand from her mouth and felt tears splash from her eyes, plus she knew that her damned nose was running. What a sight she made but she managed to squeak out; "Yes. Yes, honey, Yes."

He visibly relaxed and a broad smile spread across his beautiful face. How could he be so tense? Didn't he realize how much of a catch he was? Tory threw her arms around his neck and hugged him. The man of her dreams had just asked her to marry him. She was going to be his wife! She was going to be Victoria das Torres! She laughed against his neck, feeling his hands stroking her back, but then he pulled her back.

"I know I'm supposed to put a ring on your finger...but I wouldn't dream of trying to pick out your engagement ring. Maybe we can do that this weekend."

His brothers were there slapping him on his back and joking that he would have to do the entire thing all over again. Lee's sisters were kissing her and wiping the tears from her cheeks and then someone thrust a telephone into her hands. What the-?

She heard someone speaking rapid Portuguese and she knew that she was speaking to Lee's mother. Anxiously she covered her other ear and strained to hear the woman who was speaking to her from thousands of miles away.

"Victoria?"

"Yes, ma'am. How are you?"

There was a pleasant chuckle. "Congratulations. I am very pleased to have an addition to my family. It makes me proud and I'm so happy that Leandro has found someone special."

Tory blushed. "Thank you Ma'am. Would you like to speak to Lee?"

"Yes, please. I'll talk to you soon." Tory put her hand on Lee's upper arm and instinctively he seemed to know her touch and turned to her.

"Lee, your Mom is on the phone." His face brightened and he accepted the phone from her. The family slowly returned to their seats and the *cataplana* was served while Lee spoke in rapid Portuguese to first his mother and than his father. When he finished talking he returned the phone to

157

its rightful owner and grasped Tory's hand, holding it on his lap. She knew she had a stupid grin plastered on her face. She even heard someone say; 'Awww.'

And then she felt someone kneel between them. The smile froze on her lips when she saw Rosalind place a kiss on Lee's cheek.

"Congratulations, brother," she said quietly, a gentle smile on her lips. The conversation around the table quieted and all but stopped.

Lee patted her hand, which rested on his shoulders. "Thank you, Rosalind."

She turned to Tory next. "Please accept my congratulations."

"Of course," Tory responded, embarrassed that everyone was assessing her response for later analysis. Rosalind nodded and then turned to leave. What did it matter anymore? Lee was hers and she didn't care about any of her prior insecurities. "Would you like to join us?"

Roz stopped and glanced back at the hostess station. "Uh, I better not. I'm still working-"

"Nonsense!" Francie said. "I brought in extra help today to cover every station. Tell Armand to take over host duties and then join us, sister!"

Rosalind glanced at Tory hesitantly.

"Please do." Tory said. She felt Lee's grip tighten gently. He approved.

A smile spread across the other woman's face. "Okay."

Before long the ruckus resumed and the atmosphere once again resembled a party. They ate, they drank, they hugged and kissed and Tory had never felt more loved.

"Are you okay to drive, honey?"

"I'm okay. I stopped drinking about an hour ago." He pulled her into his arms as they headed for the car and they indulged in some PDA before she pulled back. "How about we finish this at the apartment?"

"Can you call in sick tomorrow?"

She felt the lower portion of her body tighten at his suggestion. But since being with him she had called in sick too many times and didn't want to risk a reprimand.

"Not unless I can fake up a doctor's note." He sighed.

"Then let's hurry back to your place because I want to make love to you, *querida*."

Her limbs instantly turned to liquid and she croaked out a weak; okay. It was barely 10:00 so if he wanted more time to make love that meant he was planning another lovefest. Their lovefests have been known to last upwards of 12 hours…

They hurried to the car and when she started the engine, he began scanning through his iPod. Instead of soothing Portuguese he played a Musiq Soulchild song that she adored. He reached for her hand as she drove and she peeked at him. He had a look of peace on his face.

Suddenly, there was the sound of a horn blaring loudly. Tory whipped her head around. There was a car coming at them fast. It wasn't slowing! She spun the wheel as fast and as hard as she could but not before she heard a sickening explosion as the approaching car hit them head on. It felt as if their car was being hit by a freight train.

In that moment, Tory's world slowed. She saw the two colliding cars crunching together like they were crumpling paper. And then the windshield cracked and she was seeing a beautiful kaleidoscope. The last thing she remembered is the airbag deploying and she suddenly couldn't breathe. It was as if she had been hit in the chest with a baseball bat. That's when Tory's world went black and quiet.

CHAPTER 12

Something heavy was sitting on her chest. She couldn't breathe, but when she realized that she couldn't move either the panic began to set in. Without realizing it, Tory groaned and tossed until a soothing hand covered hers. Instantly she settled. Before long she was resting and dreaming.

Much later when her eyes finally opened, Tory's first thought was that she was very tired. She blinked and tried to focus before realizing that it was night. Why did this all feel so strange? Why was she so tired? She just wanted to roll over and not think about work, to snuggle up against Lee…

Suddenly alert, Tory sat up and groaned when the sudden movement caused pain to flare up in various body parts. She looked around and realized that she was in a hospital room that was dark except for a dimmed overhead light. It didn't take longer than a few moments for her to remember that there had been a car accident, a horrible accident.

Lee!

Tory ripped the blanket and sheet from her lower body but realized that the bed railings were up. She was too dazed to figure out how to lower them, so she moved to the end of the bed but before she could drop from the end and onto the floor she was stopped by two things; one was something strapped to her face, the other was an IV connection protruding from the back of her hand.

Tory pulled the oxygen line from her face and immediately her breathing became labored. It didn't take long before she grew dizzy and lightheaded. *I'm going to blackout.* She tried to call out for help but couldn't catch her breath. What had happened to her in the accident?! Pain flared in her back and shoulder as she strained to take a breath.

I can't breathe! She reached for the oxygen and held it up to her mouth and nose, gulping big breaths. Unfortunately she was now about as weak as a newborn kitten. Lee…

Tory sank back onto the bed. *Where was he?* Her world grew black.

Tory was unsure how long she listened to the two voices speaking quietly in Portuguese. It lulled her to sleep and gave her comfort even when she knew that she should be awake because something important had happened. She had to wake up but sleep felt so good.

She sighed in distress and the voices came to an immediate stop.

"Tory?"

"Hmmm…" She moaned.

"Get the nurse. Tory? Wake up now. You've been asleep, *freira*, but now it's time to wake up."

Her eyes opened to the sight of Macey. She blinked and grimaced and then tried to sit up. Macey's face was etched in concern.

"No. You can't sit up. You have some broken ribs and a collapsed lung. "

Tory gulped down a breath, too weak to do much more than to croak out one little word. "Lee."

Macey's face dropped and she looked away. "He's okay." After a moment she looked at Tory again and her face was suddenly unreadable.

She was lying. If he was okay then he would be here now. She gave her friend a pleading look before the last of her strength faded and she either slept or blacked out.

Tory could hear her mother's voice and suddenly she was a little girl again. "Wake up Tory." Was it time for school? She was so tired. She couldn't ever remember being this tired.

"No Mama," she muttered. Someone squeezed her hand and then a brusque voice spoke.

"She's coming around. Come on Tory, you can do it."

She frowned and her eyes slowly opened. She saw the pale face of a white woman dressed in nurse's scrubs.

"There you are. Look whose here; your Mom and Dad."

Slowly she noted that Mama was holding her hand and Daddy was sitting next to her patting her arm. She took a deep breath and realized that she had an oxygen mask on. She must have tried to reach up to move it because the nurse quickly chided her.

"Tory, you can't move that." Why was this nurse talking to her like she was a child? She swallowed and focused on her parents.

"What's going on?"

Her parents looked at each other. "Tory, you were in an accident," her Mom responded.

Dear God, how could she have forgotten?! Yes, there had been an accident and while she couldn't remember the details, she knew it had been very bad. Tory tried to sit up in the narrow bed while the nurse tried to urge her back down.

"Mama, where is Lee?!"

"Lay down, honey." Daddy said with concern. The oxygen mask had slipped away from her face and he gently put it back into place.

"Tory, Lee is okay."

"Where is he then?"

"He's here in the hospital. Now you have to lie down because of your ribs." Daddy said. She allowed herself to fall back against her pillows, but she was only marginally relieved.

"I want to see him." She didn't believe them. Lee was dead, they were lying to her. She thought she was going to burst into tears but not until she got some very straight answers.

The nurse was suddenly there. "Tory, right now you are much too weak to visit him. You have a chest tube in place and you have severe cyanosis with a very big risk of cardiovascular collapse." Tory quieted. "What I'm saying is that your blood pressure is dangerously low, so low that your skin is blue. Right now you aren't able to breathe well on your own because of your collapsed lung.

"Your fiancée is recovering well, but he went through some severe trauma as well." The nurse continued. "Right now he is in the Intensive Care Unit. There was head and face trauma. He has two broken arms and a broken collarbone. Mr. Torres has some significant swelling of his brain and is in a medically induced coma. His blood pressure and vitals are very good and he is expected to make a full recovery."

Tory searched the nurse's eyes. They had to tell the truth, didn't they? They were under a Hippocratic Oath just like a doctor. So even if she was telling the truth, Tory wasn't sure if she felt relieved or horrified. He was alive and for that she was thankful. But he was in a coma trying to heal a swollen brain. His arms were broken; he needed arms and hands to see with. She closed her eyes in distress and felt her mother squeezing her hand.

"Baby, I went in to visit him and he looked very good. He's swollen, black and blue but he looked very healthy...unlike you. You have to take care of yourself, Tory. You almost died." Her mother looked at the nurse who continued for her.

"You couldn't get enough oxygen to your heart. And you have a broken rib, which can't be taped because it will further restrict your breathing. You literally cannot get up for at least another week."

"Another week?" She said hoarsely. "How long have we been here?"

"This is your second day here." The nurse moved to a machine that monitored her heart rate and blood pressure. "I'll bring you more pain medicine and leave you with your family." When the nurse left she tried to concentrate.

"There...there was a crash," she said from behind her mask.

"Try not to talk, Tory." Daddy said.

"I don't remember it," she said, ignoring his request.

Her mother sighed. "The police report says that the other driver had a blood alcohol level that was twice the legal limit. He was driving down the wrong side of the street and other cars swerved out of the way. Yours didn't. He hit you head on." She said no more.

Daddy continued. "Your blood alcohol level..." Tory gave him a quick look. "...it was well within the legal limits but you had been drinking." Was there blame there? This wasn't like when she was in college and had gone out drinking and that man had...She couldn't say anything. She knew her father didn't like for her to drink, but it wasn't like that. She was never drunk.

"We were celebrating," she tried to explain. "I wasn't drunk, Daddy."

He kissed her forehead. "Rest, honey. We'll talk more later."

"What about the other man, the one who hit us?" She suddenly and viciously hoped that he was dead.

"He's alive. It's not his first offense so he will go to jail when he's released from the hospital. I think he has a broken arm but he's in better condition than those that he hurt." Bitterly she thought that jail was too good for him, but at least he would suffer the loss of his freedom.

She closed her eyes and sighed. She was very tired. It was like she had just run a marathon and all she'd done was talk for a few minutes.

"Rest, Tory." Her mother said gently as her eyes closed. "We'll be here." Already she felt less agitated. But she couldn't wait a week before she could visit Lee. She would figure it out when she woke up. Tory slept restlessly.

The quiet sound of a discussion taking place finally pulled her once more from her slumber. Her mother was there with Francie and Kaye. Somehow that seemed all wrong; mixing her past with her present. She listened for a while feeling comforted by her mother's voice and the Portuguese accent that she had grown so accustomed to.

"How...?" she took a deep breath and felt a dull pain in her side. Three sets of eyes turned to her and then their owners converged around her bed. "What day is this?" She croaked.

"Wednesday and you are doing much better, sister." Kaye spoke. Mama gripped her hand with a smile and Francie regarded her with approval.

"She's not blue anymore." Francie said.

"No." Mama agreed.

"Brown and healthy." Kaye added. She found herself smiling.

"Is Lee better?"

Francie sat on the edge of the bed. "They are going to bring him around today. The swelling is nearly gone." Her eyes began to tear and she blinked rapidly and grabbed Tory's other hand and squeezed it gently. "I was so worried about you two. I didn't think it would turn out this well. I thought we would lose one or both of you. You both are going to be okay."

She studied her sister-in-law to be. "I want to see him. I need to see him. I want to be there when they bring him around."

"Your doctor was just here." Mama said. "He said that if you can sit up in a wheelchair then you can visit him."

"Bring the wheelchair."

Kaye smiled. "Just like an Azorean woman. We told that doctor that if he didn't give you permission to go you wouldn't get healthy AND you would find a way to sneak off and find him. Am I right, sister?"

Tory smiled, and then nodded her head. "Very true."

Francie and Kaye went to find a nurse to bring in a wheelchair, giving her alone time with her

169

mother. She asked her to brush her hair for her—silly since Lee wouldn't be able to see her anyways. Her mother took pleasure in brushing her shoulder length hair, leaving it lose although that was impractical with her being hospitalized.

"Such pretty hair." Mama said. "And you've lost so much weight, Tory. Lee must be very good for you."

"He makes me feel beautiful. He accepts everything about me." She glanced up at her mother. "It's so strange, mama. I've felt so insecure for so long and one person comes along and makes me re-evaluate how badly I've judged myself just because of my weight."

"It's society that makes us think that big can't be beautiful. You know, Tory, back in history, women built like you were put in the highest regards. In many cultures big women are in and small ones are out."

Tory didn't think the American culture would ever completely change their views on big women.

"I noticed that the women in Lee's family are all…on the bigger side." Mama was far from a big woman. She had never made Tory feel bad about her weight, but in recent years when she drew close to the three hundred pound mark, Mama and Daddy voiced their concerns and offered to help her with some type of program. That's when she became obsessed with dieting—and none of it worked for her, not until she found a man that truly didn't care. And then the weight began melting off on its own. Not completely but enough that she was comfortable in her own skin.

"Right," Tory agreed. "They aren't unhealthy, either. You should see them go, Mama. Those ladies have enough energy to run a marathon."

Francine and Kaye returned a few moments later with a nurse and wheelchair in tow. "Give me a mirror, Mama." Mama and Kaye exchanged glances and Tory immediately reached up to explore her face with trepidation. Just because Lee was blind didn't mean she was willing to give up the one thing that most people could agree on; that she had a beautiful face.

Her fingers told her that she was swollen and would be badly bruised. Mentally she prepared herself for what she would see. When her mother handed her a compact mirror she saw that she had a black eye and an angry purple bruise that covered one side of her face. The oxygen mask had been replaced with an oxygen tube and she saw that her lips were also swollen. Her skin tone was off causing her to look nearly grey. She handed the mirror back, regretting her decision to look at herself.

When the wheelchair arrived they took care getting her transported from the bed. They transferred her IV and oxygen, and then the nurse watched the monitors for a while before disconnecting her from it. She had to lay her head back and close her eyes for a few moments but then she felt better.

"I'm ready." The nurse gave her okay and Kaye wheeled her out of the room that had been home for the last 3 days.

When they arrived at the ICU ward they were met by a nurse who announced that only six visitors could go in at a time and there were already six present.

"We can switch out with four others." Kaye said.

"No, I'll just wait in the waiting area," Tory's mother said. "Just switch out with three."

Kaye wheeled her to Lee's room. Lee was lying in bed, naked from the chest up. There were monitors and tubes attached to him; helping him to breath and beeping loudly. She blinked rapidly at the sight of her beautiful man lying motionless in bed. Macey was present, as was Letiticia, who she rarely saw as she lived out of town. There was also Senna, Raphael, Rosalind and Paulo. Lee had a huge family when you factored in the seven siblings and their spouses and children. It was something that she had to become accustomed to. Now she loved it and them.

As Kaye wheeled her right next to the bed, Tory ignored everyone else as she stared at him.

He was a mess. He was cut and bruised and swollen. His arms were at his sides in heavy casts and his naked chest revealed more thick bruising. Tory realized that the bruise on his chest was from the safety belt. She reached up automatically and touched her shoulder where she knew she would have a similar one and the pain flared to life there.

There was some discussion on who would leave but all Tory could do was focus on Lee. She wanted to say *wake up. Please wake up.* But her words were trapped behind her lips. She reached out to take his hand and Kaye wheeled her even closer until she had his hand in hers. The cast ran up to his knuckles and across his palm so that his thumb poked from it. She rubbed his fingertips gently, knowing that it was very sensitive to touch, but he didn't even stir.

She forced herself not to cry, because then they might force her back to her room and she had to be here when they brought him around. She reached up and stroked his brow. He had thick bandages covering his head and she could see his thick brown curls poking through. She needed to kiss him but she couldn't and so had to settle for bringing his hand to her lips.

"I love you Lee." She whispered. "I love you. *Eu amo-te.* You are everything to me. Without you I'm lost..." she closed her eyes. "Please. I'm begging you. Please."

CHAPTER 13

Tory stayed there all morning. Francie tried to get her to eat but it wasn't until her mother came into the room threatening to force feed her did she relent. Instead of hospital food, Kaye magically produced a container of *sopa*. It was lukewarm and all meat and vegetables had been strained from it, but it was the best thing in the world and she ate the entire container.

Lee's doctors finally appeared and after studying his vitals announced that it was time to bring him out of the coma.

"We'll stop the propofol and in about 2 hours he may come around on his own. It's not totally abnormal if he doesn't and if that is the case we'll give him some drugs to essentially, 'wake him.' Any questions?" No one had questions and they began the procedure.

Tory was tired but there was no way that she could leave even though everyone encouraged her to return to her room and rest, promising to wake her up as soon as he came around. She was adamant that she wasn't going anywhere. She was holding his hand, stroking his knuckles with her thumb when there was a slight commotion at the door. She turned to see an older man and woman enter the room. Everyone jumped up and exclaimed.

She realized that it was Lee's mother and father. The older couple spared only a few moments in greeting before they joined her at the bed.

"Mr. and Mrs. Torres, I'm Tory." She said quietly.

Lee's mother gave her a wary look. His father ignored her all together. She moved her wheelchair back when they didn't say anything to her, giving them room to visit with their son. Macey wheeled her across the room and sat down in a chair next to her.

Macey was watching them sadly. The mood had changed since they arrived. Before there was quiet anticipation but now it was as if everyone was reliving the horror of the accident. Francie and Paulo went over to join their parents around Lee's bed. They talked in quiet Portuguese. Mr. Torres shook his head violently and made a cutting motion with his hands and all conversation stopped.

"What was that about?" she asked Macey who turned away and pursed her lips tightly. Tory's face dropped. It was about her.

"Macey...are your parents angry at me?" she whispered.

"Come, let's walk for a bit." Macey wheeled her out before she had a chance to object. She glanced over at the bed to see if there was any change in Lee, but he seemed exactly the same.

The two friends bypassed the waiting room where several other family members were waiting patiently for their turn to come into ICU. Mama had left to go back to the hotel and promised to return in the morning, hopefully to meet Lee-- awake and able to communicate.

They walked quietly down the corridor and to a private waiting area, which was meant to only accommodate two or three people but with the family crowding the hospital corridors there was usually five times that many people. Macey sat down and faced her. Tory recalled the first time she had set eyes on the full figured young woman that wore a perpetual smile on her face. It was the first time that she had ever considered that being overweight could also be sexy. Now Macey's pretty face was closed but sadness radiated from her. Over the months they had become friends so it was very hard to watch her now when she seemed so lost. Tory knew that Lee was her favorite sibling though she would never admit it. She had to be mindful that watching him like this wasn't just devastating to her but to them all.

"What is it, Macey?"

"There's been some talk about...about the accident and how much you had to drink."

Tory's mouth parted. "But—my dad said that the blood test indicated I was within the legal limits-"

"You were, Tory." Macey sighed and looked into the air. "Lee is so special to us. When you...or whoever is taking care of him, that person has to be even more careful with him; so that he knows that he is his own man, but doesn't realize that we are keeping him completely safe. Tory, when he gets off that bus, one of our nephews is there making sure he doesn't run into problems. We are a tight knit family but the reason we call him every single day is to make sure he is fine. We love cooking for him but if he is at the restaurant with us then we know he is alright. When he met you...we had no control over that, but it was the right thing for him." Tory was stunned at the revelation and the silent control they exuded over him.

"Tory, it takes a lot of work and patience to care for a visually impaired person-"

"I know that!"

Macey was shaking her head in denial. "You can't do things like...drink until you're impaired!" Tory's eyes widened and she looked Macey straight in her eyes.

"Is that what you think? That man was drunk and driving down the wrong side of the street! How is that my fault?"

Macey sat back, concerned etched over her face. "I didn't want you to get upset. I just wanted to tell you what the talk is within our family-"

"How can any of you think that I can be at fault?"

Macey was quiet for a moment and then she continued. "Because none of us can understand why a man driving down the wrong side of the street avoids hitting three other cars but hits yours. Tory, why didn't you pull out of the way? Everyone else did."

She caught her breath. "I tried."

"Don't be mad at me, Tory. I'm not..." Macey wiped tears from under her eyes. "I'm not saying that you are bad or did anything wrong. It's just...when it comes to Lee you have to be more, better, faster, more alert, better in control." She calmed and looked at her. "What do you think it will be like when it's not just you two but children to look after?"

"Stop it Macey." Tory said firmly. "You underestimate Lee. And I don't want to see him as the 'handicapped' person that you all obviously do. If you don't mind, I'll continue to see him as the capable man that I know him to be. He avoids accidents every single day—not because his nephew is up the block watching him, but because he's just that capable!"

Tory pulled the oxygen from her face. "That night I stopped drinking wine and switched to water so that I would continue to be sober—and at no point during the night was I ever drunk..." She suddenly paused and a look of dawning realization appeared on her face as that nights events came back to her. Tory's eyes moved to Macey's and tears appeared in her eyes, "Macy...maybe I am at fault--but not for drinking. Maybe if I hadn't taken a moment to look at your brother..." she remembered staring at the contentment on his face and thinking that she was responsible for putting that look on his face. She remembered feeling amazed that he found her to be someone special enough to choose. He chose her. In that moment she had been more proud than she could ever remember. Tory swallowed and shook her head and returned the oxygen to its position beneath her nose. God this really was her fault...

Macey was crying now too. *"Tens que pedir desculpa,* Tory! There is nobody better for my brother than you. You are the one that was God-given to him, I'm convinced of that. Please forgive me for ever doubting you. You are Lee's woman in every way."

Tory stared at her in surprise as tears filled her eyes again. "But I just sat here and told you that I probably caused your brother's accident-" Tory was shaken to her core at the thought that anything she had done could have contributed to Lee's pain. Her daddy had alluded to drinking and driving. Stupid. She hadn't been drunk but it was still stupid! And then she looks at him while driving...how long; two seconds, five? More? How could she have been so careless?!

"Tory I can see it on your face," Macey gripped her hand tightly. "I have put this self doubt in you and now I have no doubt that no one will ever care for him more than you. It was an accident Tory; an accident that is no fault of yours, an accident that happened on the day of your engagement, an accident that was brought on by a series of events that you could not foresee."

"We better go back." Tory finally said.

Macey stood and then paused. "Can you forgive me? I ask you this woman to woman."

"I...there's nothing to forgive. You told me what was on the minds of your family and I appreciate your honesty even if it was hard for me to hear." She reached out and took Macey's hand. "The honesty within your family is what I most love about you. I'll explain this to each and every one of you if that's what I need to do, but for now, it's the last thing I care about. Okay? I just want to go back and be with Lee."

Macey nodded and then began wheeling her back to ICU. A little girl about 12 met them in the corridor.

"Aunt Macey! Uncle Lee is waking up!"

CHAPTER 14

Macey and Tory headed for the ICU. None of the family was in the ICU waiting area so it appeared that everyone was now allowed into Lee's room to witness his awakening.

Tory squeezed the armrest of the wheelchair. She knew that there was a chance that Lee's brain could have been injured even though no one talked about it. She saw everyone crowding around the bed and Macey pushed their way through so that she was front and center.

"Mr. Torres, can you hear me?" One of the doctors asked. There were interns, doctors and nurses all crowded into the room--not to mention a roomful of relatives and a fiancée in a wheelchair. But no one moved, no one barely even breathed.

"Mmm…" Came the whisper of a groan from the bed. Tory squeezed her hands into fists. Was that a groan of pain, or was it just his confirmation? She saw that his eyes were still closed but his breathing was different and he was moving his limbs restlessly.

"Mr. Torres, I'm Dr. Hendrix. Can you hear me?" There was no response and soon Lee began to quiet. Oh no…Dr. Hendrix tried for several more minutes before he paused and looked around the room. "He's not responding to my voice. Someone else speak to him. Maybe if he recognizes the voice he'll come around."

Several people turned to Tory. She reached for his hand but before she could even touch him Rosalind's voice could be heard from where she was standing on the opposite side of his bed.

"Leandro, Listen to my voice. You need to wake up, brother."

Tory's mouth parted in surprise and outrage. She didn't notice that several other people in the room had mimicked her expression but then Lee's head turned in Rosalind's direction although his eyes remained closed. His breathing calmed and he seemed to be awake and listening.

Rosalind continued talking but now in Portuguese, encouraging words but words that Tory was hopeless to understand. Simultaneously, both women took one of his hands. Their eyes met and there was no pretense; the dislike was evident on both women's faces.

Rosalind turned her attention back to Lee and continued to speak to him in soft Portuguese. And then suddenly he was squeezing her hand. Everyone gasped in excitement. Rosalind's face broke into a beatific smile.

"That's right, Lee. I'm here. I'm here."

Tory was confused with the need to jump out of her chair and beat Rosalind about the head and face, but she was also excited to see him waking. *Come on baby*…she begged silently.

"Please, baby…" She whispered.

A frown flitted across Lee's face and he slowly turned his head in Tory's direction.

"*Querida*…" He mumbled.

A short, relieved laugh gushed from her lips and tears were in her eyes. "Yes, I'm here."

He frowned and grimaced and then his eyes opened slightly.

"Where am I?"

"He's awake," someone exclaimed. Mrs. Torres nudged Rosalind out of the way to take her son's hand. Ah, so she was just naturally rude. Then Tory didn't feel quite so bad about the earlier snub. Rosalind looked unhappy about being replaced but moved aside to give Mrs. Torres room. Again, Portuguese was spoken and Lee listened quietly and although Tory was curious she was more relieved that Lee was alternately squeezing her hand and stroking her knuckle with his thumb.

He suddenly interrupted his mother and turned to face Tory.

"Tory, are you hurt?" Ah, so she had told him about the accident.

She removed the oxygen. "I'm okay honey, I broke a rib…and I have a collapsed lung." Lee pulled his hand from his mother's grasp and grimaced as he tried to reach up to touch her. He couldn't because of the IV and monitoring equipment, not to mention the bulky cast, so he was unable to see if she was okay.

"You have two broken arms, honey," she explained. "But you're awake and you're going to be okay now." He flexed his fingers.

Dr. Hendrix spoke. "Mr. Torres, I'm Dr. Hendrix. If you don't mind I'd like to ask you some questions."

"Why?"

"Well, we want to make sure that you haven't experienced any damage to your brain and we'll need to be sure that your central nervous system is functioning the way it should." He turned to the crowd of people. "Unfortunately I'm going to have to ask everyone to leave now. But we shouldn't be long and if you'll return to the family waiting area I'll consult with you when I'm finished."

Lee frowned again. "Is everyone here?" Everyone made sure to let him know that they were present—and it wasn't quietly. He bit his lip lightly. "I'd like for my mother, father and Tory to stay, please. I need them to stay." He clutched Tory's hand and reached for his mother's with the other.

Everyone else left noisily, voicing their disappointment at being asked to leave. While this happened, Tory stood and pressed her face against his neck. It hurt her back and shoulders and took her breath away when she came out of the wheelchair but she couldn't stop herself. She had to allow her lips to touch him. He closed his eyes again and leaned into her.

"Tory," he sighed and she could both feel and see the anxiety leaving his body. Mr. and Mrs. Torres watched her and it took a long time for her to realize it but when she did she watched them just as closely as they watched her. Something strange and surprising happened then. Both parents simultaneously smiled.

She was guarded when she nodded a silent greeting. She had already tried to introduce herself and was ignored. She wouldn't be so quick to make the same mistake.

Mrs. Torres moved and was suddenly standing next to her. "Tory, sit back down. You need to stay healthy." She urged her back to her chair and adjusted the oxygen back beneath her nose. Tory gave her a surprised look. "You're a good girl." She touched her cheek and looked deeply into her eyes. "You love my son."

"Very much so."

Mrs. Torres smiled. Tory was just confused. How did these people just arbitrarily dislike and then like someone?! She didn't get it but was pleased the tides had changed in her favor...at

186

least for now. Soon she would have to tell them about the accident and take blame for her part in it. But what she wouldn't do is lay claim to driving impaired, unless it was impairment due to admiring your gorgeous fiancée.

Dr. Hendrix and his team of doctors put Lee through comprehensive tests and then announced that he seemed very healthy despite being a bit groggy.

"I have a headache," he announced.

"Of course," Dr. Hendrix replied. "I'll have pain medicine placed in your IV."

"When can we leave?"

The doctor's eyes flitted to Tory and then he raised a brow. "I'd like to monitor you for the next 24 hours and if all is well then I see no reason why you shouldn't be able to go home tomorrow. I'm not your fiancée's doctor but I will confer with him."

Lee squeezed her hand gently and then a moment later the doctors left to speak to the other members of the family.

"Where are you staying?" Lee said to his parents once the room was empty.

Lee's father responded in Portuguese but Lee interrupted him. "Daddy, speak in English, please. Tory doesn't understand yet." She smiled at the word 'yet.' The older man gave her an apologetic smile.

"We forget easily."

"I'm not surprised. You haven't been to the states in years, I understand."

"We speak English on the island but not much." Mrs. Torres responded. "We're staying with Raphael and Fiona-"

"Well I would like for you to stay with me while you're in town. We have an extra bedroom that I just use as an office." *We*...She hadn't had much time to absorb the fact that their lives were now one so of course it was we.

"Is that okay with you Tory?" Mrs. Torres asked.

"Yes, definitely. Lee and I don't live together yet. But even if we did that would be fine with me!" She said quickly.

"We'll let you two visit," she said but before leaving she and Mr. Torres leaned down and kissed him and then both of them kissed Tory. She was a little uncomfortable but only because she didn't know if these people would decide that they didn't like her anymore once they talked with the rest of the family and Rosalind.

"It was nice to finally meet you." She said politely.

When they were gone Tory stood up again and leaned into Lee, her lips finding his neck and staying there so that she could inhale him. He reached up and rubbed her arm, careful of the cast. He turned so that he could explore her with his hands. His fingers moved slowly over her face finding every bit of swelling. He made a sound of distress when he discovered her oxygen line.

"Are you in a wheelchair?" She nodded without answering. He moved over to the far side of the narrow bed and moved his covers back. "Lay with me." A smile tugged at her lips. It wasn't as easy as it seemed but a few moments later she was lying nestled against his side with her arm thrown across his body.

"Are you sure you're okay?"

"I am now that I know you are." She felt him smile.

"We're okay, *bela*."

CHAPTER 15

Tory was anxious when her parents came the next day to take her home and they finally got a chance to be introduced to her fiancée.

Lee had been moved to a private room and he was never alone; far from it. Everyone present greeted her warmly, but she knew that some among them might have suspicions about her now. She put that out of mind as she kissed Lee's smiling face.

"Mama, Daddy, I want you to meet my fiancée, Lee." Saying that word sent a shiver down her spine.

Lee held out his hand and her father gripped it firmly and shook. "It's a pleasure to meet you sir." He shook her mother's hand. "I'm sorry that our meeting is under such unpleasant circumstances."

"It's fine, honey. I'm just happy that you two are safe."

Francie ushered everyone out of the room to give them time to visit and they talked for a few minute before her parents retreated to get her checked out of the hospital.

Reluctantly she returned to her room to get her things together. Yesterday evening she had tried to convince everyone that she would be okay returning to Lee's home to take care of him, and she thought Lee would support her efforts, but it was him that finally convinced her that she needed to return to her apartment, stay in bed and allow her mother to take care of her until she got the thumbs up from her doctor.

Deep down she knew that he was probably right, but it hurt her feelings that he wouldn't let her come home with him; that he actually said no to her. While her parents got her checked out and made sure that everything was billed to her insurance company, Macey helped her prepare to leave her room. Tory was preoccupied, wanting to tell Lee goodbye one more time but she had just left him so that was dumb. It's just that if she was going to be on bed rest, she wouldn't see him for days.

"So..." Macey began. Tory gave her a quick look.

"What?"

"No comment on how scandalous Rosalind acted yesterday?"

"Ugh. No comment."

Macey chuckled. "For the record, she didn't gain any points when she jumped in and started talking to my comatose brother just when his fiancée was about to. That was your place, not hers!"

"Agreed." She stared at Macey. "Are there people that still blame me?"

Macey looked away. "There isn't a really good translation for this. Some have placed the responsibility of his condition on you without blaming you for creating the accident—but as a contributor to it." She looked at Tory then. "I've told people my opinion and they listen. I think that maybe they just…doubt you. But no one doubts your commitment and your love for Lee."

"I'm sure Roz is one on the other team."

"I guess you could say that." Macey replied with a mirthless grin.

"And your mother and father?"

"My parents don't want anything or anybody stressing out Lee. Mama already went off on Roz and told her not to start up around him. She was not happy with the stunt she pulled. Roz tried to say that she thought he might respond to Portuguese since it's in his heart." Macey rolled her eyes. "Mama said it was between you and Lee and that shut it down."

Tory felt a smile tugging at her lips as she found herself liking his parent's more and more. She had certainly hoped to make a better impression. Being accused of nearly killing ones son did not make for the best first impression. So the upside was that she knew they didn't totally hate her. But the downside was that now she knew they were talking about her behind her back. She sat down on the edge of the bed suddenly tired. It was wonderful when the clan was all on her side—but having them against her was unsettling.

But she knew that she would go up against any of them if she had to. They were not going to push her away from the man she loved. She had no doubt about that, but she did worry about one thing; If they didn't eventually accept her as Lee's woman and trust that she would be there for him in all ways, could they influence him against her? She knew how much he valued his family...

She just wanted to be there! To balance everything so that Roz couldn't stack the cards against her.

"Don't worry about this. Just be yourself, Tory. You don't have to try to convince anyone of anything." She nodded knowing that Macey was a good ally and friend. She trusted her, mostly because she had been woman enough to tell her face to face what was going on.

Back at her apartment Tory got settled into her bed even though bed was the last place she wanted to be. There was tons of work that needed to be done; the spare bedroom needed to be straightened up so that her parents could move into it. The refrigerator needed cleaning because something had spoiled. The trash needed taken out and Daddy wouldn't even allow her to take care of the insurance adjuster. He announced that she would be able to pick up a new car by the end of the week. With a sigh she finally decided to just relent and relax in bed. Within 5 minutes Tory was deep asleep.

The next few days moved very slowly for Lee and Tory. They spent hours talking on the phone and telling the other how much they were missed.

On the second day Lee seemed preoccupied but still attentive and happy to talk to her. After about an hour of talking he spoke hesitantly.

"Tory...on the night of the accident what actually happened?"

Her heart slammed against her tender ribcage. "How much do you remember?"

"Honestly, not very much. The last thing I remember is holding your hand in the car. I don't even remember the accident at all, just waking up in the hospital."

She wished that she could be so lucky. Sometimes she dreamed about a car driving right at them, always in slow motion so that it gave her enough time to realize that there was absolutely nothing that she could do to save them. Once the dream showed an alternative ending in which Lee hadn't survived. Seeing him like that, even if it was just a dream, had shaken her to her core. After having known a love like the one she shared with Lee, Tory knew that she could not bear to lose him.

She sighed. "We were driving. Another man approaching us was driving in the wrong lane. He never slowed. He just hit us straight on."

There was a long pause. "Did you swerve out of the way?"

"I tried to. I turned the wheel fast but I…it wasn't fast enough."

Another long pause. "He only hit us? Do you know how long he was driving down the wrong side of the street?"

"I don't know, baby. For me, it was as if he just appeared out of nowhere. I…I was driving, holding your hand. I turned to look at you and…it was just for a second. I heard a horn blow and I looked back and there he was." Tory closed her eyes, feeling guilt, shame and fear of his reaction.

"Okay," he said simply.

"I'm sorry Lee-"

"It's okay baby. It wasn't you that caused the accident. It was that man. He has to appear in court on Friday. I don't know if you want to go or not-"

"I don't! No, I don't want to."

"It's okay. I don't either. But I will write a letter and I want you to as well; for the prosecution, okay?"

"Okay, I'll do that. What are you going to say in yours?"

"I'm going to tell him that his thoughtlessness nearly killed two innocent people and that I hope

195

he gets the maximum sentence. My sense of touch is my life. I can't transcribe Braille if I can't feel with my fingers. I can't see you or others without touch. He very nearly cost me my arms. You know, Tory, if it wasn't for the fact that we chose a 'safe' car, we would not have survived. Carlos said the car had no front end but the rest of it was intact, almost perfect. We were in a safety cage surrounded by deployed airbags. He said he's never seen anything like it."

Carlos had been kind enough to get their personal effects out of the car. She wondered if he was one of the ones that no longer liked her. Tears suddenly appeared in her eyes and she grew quiet.

"Are you okay, honey? I'm sorry Tory, I didn't mean to upset you."

"No, it's just that I know how close we came to not making it. I don't know what I would do without you Lee."

"You will never have to know that, *querida*."

"You can never say never…" Look how close they had come.

"Yes I can! Stop it Tory. There is no looking back, only forward, do you understand?"

She was surprised at his brusque tone. He never talked harsh to her.

"Y-yes."

"Good. I'm not going to lose you and you're not going to lose me."

She relaxed. "Yes."
"I love you." He said.
"Eu amo-te."
She heard his soft chuckle. *"Eu amo-te."*

Friday was a day of anticipation for both Lee and Tory. After her check-up she was to meet him at his place. Daddy took her to pick up the replacement car early that morning and then rode in the passenger seat despite her assurance that she didn't need him to. Mama wordlessly drove their rental car to the doctor's office to meet them.

Her father was wonderful. He never mentioned the fact that she was shaking like a leaf as soon as she got in behind the wheel. He never scolded her for driving too slow—so slow, in fact, that it could have caused another accident! But after a few miles she was comfortable again.

When they got out of the car to go to her doctor's appointment she threw her arms around her father's neck and kissed his cheek.

"What's that for?" He smiled.

"Because..." She thought about the fact that a few short days ago she nearly lost her life and might not have ever seen her Mom and Dad again. "Because you are the best father in the world."

He snorted. "If you say so." But he took her hand and they headed to her appointment hand in hand just like he used to do when she was a kid.

Tory received a clean bill of health and a reminder that after-care for someone with a lung injury was to be taken very seriously and followed strictly. She was strongly reminded that by not following the rules she was at risk for cardiac arrest; a heart attack.

Mama stopped her as they left the building. "Daddy and I are going to catch an earlier plane out. We already have our things in the trunk."

"What?" Tory frowned. "You don't have to do that. I'll be back home later tonight-"

Mama chuckled. "Tory, you don't have to come home for us." Her cheeks warmed and she knew that she was blushing. "You and Lee haven't seen each other in days and I'm sure that you'd much rather be with him." Mama patted her hand. "Besides, you're well enough and Daddy and I need to go home."

"Well..." she sighed in distress, not wanting her mother and father to think she was ungrateful. "You didn't even get a chance to really meet Lee. I thought we'd all go out to dinner or something tomorrow."

Mama kissed her cheek and then headed for their car. "We'll be back up for the wedding."

Tory smiled and hugged her arms. Yes, she was getting married. Daddy kissed the top of her head. You call us if you need anything, okay baby girl?"

"Okay, Daddy. But I'll be okay."

He seemed reluctant to leave. "I know you will be." She knew how difficult it was on her parents. First there were the events that happened when she was in college and now this. He finally joined Mama at the car.

"I love you!" She called. They beeped the horn and were gone. For a moment she felt sad but then remembered that she was getting ready to see her man and she dashed to her car.

When Tory reached Lee's building she was not happy to see that the street was lined with familiar cars. Shit, that meant that the Torres clan was out in full force. She refused to admit to being horny. It seemed wrong to think about sex when she had a hole in her lung and Lee's arms were in casts and both of them were still black and blue. But she missed him like crazy and maybe it wasn't so much that she needed the release—she just needed the intimacy. She pulled into the underground parking garage. She saw a second car there with a rental license and knew it was his mom and dad's.

Lee evidently heard the elevator because he was standing there waiting for her as soon as the cage door went up.

"Hi, Baby!" She said happily. A broad smile came over his face and he opened his arms allowing her to step into them. Even though his arms were now sheathed in hard plaster up to his elbows, being held by him felt amazing. She was reluctant to leave the comfortable space except for the fact that the large living room was filled with onlookers. How is it that Mama could figure out that they needed alone time but these people couldn't?

She smiled at them and they suddenly converged on her, asking her how she was doing, telling her that she looked a lot better, kissing and hugging her. Everyone was very nice but she couldn't help wondering which ones disliked her.

She knew she wasn't being fair. Questioning her ability to care for Lee did not equate to disliking her…well except for one person. Her eyes locked on to Rosalind who made sure to stay on the other end of the room. Mr. and Mrs. Torres greeted her equally as enthusiastically. She was ushered to the living room where Francine insisted she sit down before her lung opened back up. Tory bit the inside of her cheek so she wouldn't laugh but she did sit down and Lee sat down right next to her.

"How was your appointment?" Lee asked and everyone quieted to listen. Tory cleared her voice.

"I'm doing well. The doctor just told me not to overdo it. I'm going to go back to work Monday." Lee made a face. "And I picked up the replacement car."

Lee ran his hand through his curls. There was a patch missing just above his left ear but it couldn't detract from his model good looks. As Tory watched him, she felt the breath stick in her lungs and for the millionth time she wondered how she had been so lucky.

"Tory, I think you should take some time off from work."

She gave him a surprised look. "Really?"

"Lee's got 2 broken arms..." Senna said and she suddenly knew who else was on the Does-not-like-Tory-list. She looked from Senna to Lee who had a strange look on his face. He was shaking his head slightly and his brow was knit.

"I don't need you to take off for me. I want you to take off for you." Tory glanced around the room watching the tide turn against her.

"I need to work, honey...don't I?" She didn't know a lot about his finances. She knew he was more than comfortable in the financial department but now he would have someone else to take care of. She had a college loan to pay off and they had just bought a fifty thousand dollar car.

"We'll talk about it later," he exhaled anxiously. "Excuse me." He got up and she watched him in surprise as he tentatively made his way across the room. She noted that he moved slower, his arms out before him as if he was no longer familiar with his surroundings. Just as he reached the corridor that led to the bathroom he stumbled over a toy that one of the kids had left on the floor. No less than 5 people jumped to his assistance before catching themselves and holding back. Lee caught himself before he fell but he kicked the toy in uncharacteristic anger.

As soon as Lee was in the bathroom, Senna stalked into the kitchen muttering to herself in Portuguese.

Macey frowned and sat down next to Tory. "Lee is not adjusting well to his injuries."

"What do you mean?"

Macey glanced at the corridor and continued quickly. "He's lost. It's like he no longer has his confidence. He hasn't left the apartment even to come to the restaurant. Tory, maybe you can help him."

She nodded quickly as Lee returned slowly to the living room. Everyone mingled and talked but she now saw that they watched him closely. He paused a few short steps from the couch and held out his hand tentatively. It broke her heart that he had to think before coming to sit on the couch that he used to drop onto; the very same couch that he would push her down onto while he hovered above her kissing her from top to bottom. Tory stood up and reached for his hand. He grasped them and only then would he move to resume his seat on the couch.

He sat down quietly and Tory intertwined her fingers with his, holding him and feeling his fear and uncertainty. Dear God, what had that accident taken from him?

CHAPTER 16

Dinner was a strange affair. The family was animated and friendly. They talked, laughed, ate and drank, but beneath it ran a tension. Eyes darted around, secret communications ran from person to person and everything seemed forced. If Lee picked up on it she couldn't tell. He seemed distant and preoccupied.

"Are you ok, honey?" She whispered.

He put on a quick smile. "I'm okay." She could see him force down a few bites of food but for the most part he just sat quietly and observed. She needed to talk to him, privately. But Tory realized that even after dinner when the family would make their way back to their own homes, she and Lee still wouldn't be alone because his mother and father was staying here.

At the moment, sex was the last thing on her mind. She had to find out what he was going through. Could it be that he blamed her for the accident? Had Rosalind gotten to him? They've had days with him and obviously they could have influenced him.

By eight the house was empty and the dishes cleaned. No one would allow her to help with the

204

cleaning even though with many hands it took only a few minutes. When the last person had exited Lee sighed and Tory could see the strain on his face. Something was definitely up. Mr. and Mrs. Torres announced that they would turn in for the night although it was barely eight o'clock. She appreciated the gesture and wished them a warm good night.

When they were alone he pulled her into his arms and hugged her, more like he hung onto her. It was the first time that they'd been along in days. She buried her face into his chest and clung to him, listening to the sound of his heart drumming rapidly in his chest.

"Lee," she looked up, still holding on to him. "What's wrong, tell me?"

A frown flitted across his handsome face. "I'm just happy you're here. Let's just...go to bed. I'm exhausted."

"Okay," She replied, but she didn't intend to let it go.

She went into the bathroom and remembered they weren't alone and shut the door before peeing. She was brushing her teeth when something slammed into the door. Tory dropped her toothbrush and with a mouthful of toothpaste darted to the closed door and opened it.

Lee was in pajama bottoms and a t-shirt. He was rubbing his head and Tory gasped because she could see a lump forming over his right eye.

"Oh baby, I'm so sorry!"

"I-no, it's not your fault. I should have known it was closed. I could—the sound of the water was muffled. I just wasn't thinking."

"No, it was my fault."

"Tory." He said with finality and moved past her into the bathroom. He walked slowly, arms held out slightly in front of him until he reached the sink. He got his toothbrush and felt around for the toothpaste and then began brushing his teeth. She quietly joined him at the basin and finished up.

Afterwards she followed him into the bedroom. She found her nightshirt and then stripped out of her clothes and pulled it on over her head. She climbed into bed with him where he was propped up against his pillows.

After a few moments where neither moved or talked she finally spoke.

"Talk to me...because I feel like you're...mad at me."

"I'm not," he said quickly but he didn't look at her, or at least in her direction.

"Then talk to me baby-"

"What in the hell do you want me to say, Tory?!" he glared in her direction. "I don't fucking know what you want me to say."

She was so surprised that any response froze in her throat. He had never cursed at her before—not ever. He had never ever raised his voice at her.

"Do you want me to leave?"

"No," he said quickly. He reached out and stroked her arms. "I'm sorry. I am just so stressed and—but I want you to know that I'm happy you're here. I thought I was going to go crazy wanting you here."

And now I'm here and you cuss me? "Stressed about what?"

He released her, something unreadable on his face. He lay back facing straight up. "I don't know. That's the problem. I just don't know." He turned to her. "I just feel like…"

She lay on her side facing him. "Like what?" she prodded gently.

"Like my entire life was just an illusion." He paused and then seemed to stare right into her eyes. "I thought I was in control of it, but I'm not. I'm just a…passenger. I have no control over anything."

"Baby…" she began, alarmed by his words. "You are the most capable man that I've ever met. There is not a day that goes by that I'm not in constant awe of you. You are a blind man that has accomplished more than most sighted people. You are funny, sexy, talented, and smart--but most of all you are confidant." Tory watched the intense expression on his face and hoped that he was listening and believing that she meant every word.

His expression was uncertain. "Is that what you really see Tory?"

"Yes!"

He paused and then leaned forward and kissed her forehead — she wasn't sure if he was going for her mouth but either was okay.

"Thank you. I needed that," he whispered.

"Don't doubt yourself. Don't doubt what I feel for you." She opened and then closed her mouth. Suddenly she knew she had to say what was on her mind. "I know that...some people in your family blame me for you getting hurt-"

"What the fuck? Who told you that? Macey? She is a fucking busybody." He said angrily.

"Lee!" His outburst surprised her.

"No, I'm sick of people getting in our business!" He sat up in bed and ran his hand through his hair. "I understand their concern, especially under the circumstances. But..." He turned back to her and reached out for her hand. "I'm sorry, Tory. I'm just so..."

"Stressed?" He didn't say anything. "Lee don't be mad at Macey. I picked up on the tension. She just explained it to me. She is on my side. She is on *our* side."

He relaxed. "I know she is. "It's Senna and Leticia that are starting shit."

"And Rosalind."

He shook his head. "Rosalind?"

"Yeah. She hates me."

"Baby, that incident was a long time ago. She's not said anything against you. As a matter of fact she told me that she hoped you two could be friends."

Tory sat up in bed and made a humph noise. That slick bitch! And he was falling for it. Of course she wasn't talking about her in front of Lee. She would do it behind their back and try to fuel the flames against her.

"Rosalind can use as many friends as possible right now." Lee continued. "She and Brice just separated-"

"What?" Tory's voice was a whisper.

"Yeah, and she's not taking it well."

Tory felt the blood drain from her face. Rosalind intended to come after Lee and she intended to do it in the 'correct' way — a way that his family couldn't find fault with.

When Tory awoke the next morning she noticed three things; the bed beside her was empty, the smell of good food, and the sound of Portuguese music playing from the other room.

Last night she had gone to sleep in Lee's arms. Even with the casts it was comfortable. He had planted another kiss on her forehead and that time she knew it wasn't an accident. He had fallen asleep quickly and she couldn't find fault in that. He had told her before that he was exhausted.

Tory sat up in bed and checked the clock. Oh my God it was nearly eleven o'clock! How could she have slept so late? They had been in bed by nine o'clock which meant that she'd slept over 12 hours. She scrambled out of bed and pulled on her robe. She rubbed her hands through her unruly hair and hurried out of the room.

Mr. and Mrs. Torres were standing at the computer that had been moved from the spare room to the living room. They were oohing and aaahing at something he was showing them until Mrs. Torres turned to her.

"*Ola*, Tory," She gave her a knowing smile. But nothing had happened last night!

Mr. Torre's eyes scanned her attire and his brow arched. She made sure that her robe was closed.

"Uh, good morning," she said.

Lee minimized the computer screen and with a broad grin he walked over to her. She was pleased that he didn't have to hold his arms out and that he moved confidently the way he had before the accident. She felt a rush of guilt when she saw the purple bruise standing out prominently over his eye. But he was all smiles and didn't seem to notice it at all.

"Morning? I'm sorry to tell you that you missed morning and are about to greet the afternoon." He pulled her into his arms and kissed her lovingly. She pulled back because his parents were staring.

"Why didn't you wake me?" She mumbled to him.

"My mother said that you needed your rest."

Oh, well she couldn't argue with that.

"Are you hungry? You missed breakfast but lunch is nearly ready."

She grimaced. Ugh, food was not tops on her list. She just wanted coffee and a piece of Danish...if that. But she knew that if Mrs. Torres was anything like her mother, she would insist she eat well in order to build up her strength. She smiled and lied, saying that she was a little hungry.

"*Feijoada de vaca* will be ready soon."

Tory gestured to the bathroom. "I'm going to get showered. I'll be back."

After showering and dressing, she checked her messages and saw that Mama had called. She listened to the message; they had arrived safely. She felt guilty for not calling to check and then further guilty when Mama reminded her to use her Incentive spirometer to help with her breathing.

She hated the thing. She was supposed to use it three times a day to help strengthen and open up her lungs. But it made her feel lightheaded and dizzy and so she would skip it anytime she could. She hadn't even brought it with her.

She decided to send Mom a quick text telling her that she was happy she had seen them and would call her later. She didn't mention the spirometer.

When she returned to the living room the table was set and Lee and his father were sitting in chairs watching something on his computer. Oh what a surprise; soccer, she though with a wry grin. She had discovered that Lee and his family were demented over the sport. The fact that he didn't own a television set didn't stop him from keeping up with his favorite team. He could tune into foreign channels via computer. At that very moment the two men cheered happily at some unknown event. She placed her hand on his shoulder and kissed him on the cheek from behind.

"Mmmm," he said simply, pausing long enough to receive it.

"*Cerveja?*"

"Yes, thanks, honey."

Tory gave Mr. Torres a quick smile. "I'll bring you one, too."

"*Obrigado*, Tory. Thank you," he responded with an appreciative smile.

She went into the kitchen and saw Mrs. Torres putting slices of fresh baked bread onto a plate and singing a Portuguese song. Tory knew it. It was one by Amália Rodrigues who was like the Elvis Presley of Portuguese music. Whenever Lee played music by her, his vibe would change. It was like the way she felt when she played a song like Yearning for Your Love by The Gap Band or Serpentine Fire by Earth Wind and Fire. Listening to music from her parent's generation made her feel good and it was the same with him. Wanting to know more, Tory and Lee began to play those special songs for each other until each now had favorites from the others history. The one Mrs. Torres now sang was one of them.

Lee's mother was an excellent singer and Tory couldn't help but stand there for a moment listening. She caught herself when she saw Tory and laughed, clutching her chest.

"Sorry, that was beautiful," Tory apologized.

Mrs. Torres waved away her words. "Old music for an old woman."

"I like *fado*." Tory moved to the refrigerator for beer.

"Oh, Tory! You know *fado* music?" She peeked around the refrigerator door unsure why that would surprise her.

"Yes, ma'ame. It's like...Portuguese blues." She closed the refrigerator door with two beers in tow. "I also like that song you were singing; *Povo que lavas no rio.*" Folk who bathe in the river. When Lee interpreted the lyrics for her it made her think of Strange Fruit by Billie Holiday. She was instantly enraptured by the song;

Folk who wash in the river, who with your axe prepare, the planks of my coffin, there will be those who defend you, who'll buy your sacred ground, but no, not your life.

She left the kitchen calling over her shoulders. "I'll be back in a minute, Mrs. Torres to help you." She didn't see the look of surprise on her soon-to-be-mother in law's face.

CHAPTER 17

After lunch Mr. and Mrs. Torres decided to do some visiting and asked Tory and Lee if they wanted to join them.

The couple was sitting on the couch holding hands. Lee shrugged. "I think we'll pass."

"Yeah." Tory agreed. "I'm in the mood to kick off my shoes and plant myself on this couch."

"Okay, kids. We'll see you tonight. *Até logo.*" Mr. Torres called and they disappeared into the elevator. Lee perked his ears and listened until the elevator reached the ground floor. He got up and moved to the elevator and listened. When he turned he had a smile on his face.

"*Vem aqui,*" he held out one hand to her in invitation. *Come here.*

*Oooo…*Tory came to her feet and sauntered over to him. The apartment was quiet and she knew that he was listening to each step of her slippered feet against the stone floor. She felt a flutter deep down in the pit of her stomach and then it blossomed and spread electric fingers throughout her body.

She stopped just a mere foot in front of him. His arms snaked out and gripped her about the

215

waist and she thought; *that's right baby. I'm right here*...Strong hands ran lovingly over the curve of her ass, pausing there to stroke and explore her. Her hands moved around his strong shoulders, careful of his bruising and healing collarbone. Lee closed the space between them and she could feel his hard muscular frame as it pressed against her much softer flesh.

"Baby, I missed you," she sighed. Lee's head lowered and he suddenly had her bottom lip gripped between his. His tongue pushed into her mouth and he kissed her passionately, nearly crushing her lips in the process.

She no longer remembered to be careful of his bruises and she held onto him tightly, pressing her body against his, discovering that he was more than aroused; he was unyieldingly hard. She couldn't help it, she rolled her hips against his cock, feeling wanton and weak with desire.

"I missed you..." she gasped. "Please baby..."

Lee groaned and suddenly gripped her ass and lifted her. Her legs went around his hips and for a moment all he could do was stand there and hold her in his plaster casted arms.

"I love you. I love you so much, Tory. I can't stop thinking about how close I came to losing you and there was nothing that I could do-"

"Shh," she kissed his face and ran her hands through his hair. "You took care of us, don't you see? You bought a car with safety in mind and because of it we made it. That was all you, baby. I would have bought a hooptie."

He chuckled and planted kisses on her face. After a while he sighed and just stood there holding her in his arms. They touched foreheads and stayed that way until he lowered her back to her feet. "Let's go to bed."

They walked hand in hand and once in the bedroom Lee stopped her before she could undress. "No. I want to do it, *bela*." She shivered as he lifted her blouse above her head. His fingers moved to lightly touch her breasts, tracing the bra where it met her flesh.

Tory closed her eyes, relishing his gentle touch. Now blind, she experienced each sensation with a renewed intensity. She felt his fingers glide between her breasts and down her abdomen. Slowly he moved past her belly button, trailing down to her jeans. Tory knew that she was breathing hard and fast. She stood there unmoving and felt Lee unbutton her pants and drag the zipper down slowly. He stepped closer to her, his body pressed against hers lightly. She felt his hands in her panties, pushing them and her pants down in one fluid motion and she couldn't help the sharp intake of breath.

He bent and had her step out of them and now all she was wearing was the bra. He reached around and unhooked it, letting it drop to the floor. His hands moved up the sides of her body, seeming to rediscover each curve. He left no part of her torso untouched and when he discovered the bandage, beneath which the tube had pierced her lung, his brow drew together and he placed a tentative kiss there before moving on. He found the bruise on her shoulder and kissed it and so that he wouldn't miss kissing any injury he kissed every inch of her body until she could take no more.

"Please…" she begged breathlessly.

He raised his head and looked at her. "Please, what?"

"Please," she bit her lip her eyes bright. "Put it in me. Make me cum, make love to me, fuck me—I don't care! I just want to feel you inside of me!"

"Fuck…" he lifted her and carried her to the bed, lying her down carefully. Then he swiftly removed his clothes, grimacing once when he raised his arms above his head to remove his shirt. When he was naked, standing over her in beautiful perfection, Tory moaned in anticipation. He was so beautiful. He'd often called her beautiful, but he was. He was perfect. He was hers.

"*Tu és tão lindo,*" she whispered.

He lowered himself carefully on top of her. "You are the beautiful one, and you don't even realize it. My beautiful Tory." He brought himself up until he was poised to enter her and she suddenly felt him pushing into her. She was slick and ready but for a moment she felt that he might over fill her. But then her body relaxed and closed around his girth. He sighed and uttered a word that she didn't know; whether it was Portuguese or some mixture of a groan and a word she just didn't know. His hips began its slow roll and then it was her that made non-existent words.

He increased his pace and Tory's legs encased his body while her hips slid up and down in rhythm to his pumping hips.

Oh god! It was so good. She was liquid…she was the epitome of all sensation. She was a neuron that transmitted and received every chemical and electric signal in both her and Lee's bodies! The rising tide of passion was overpowering—strong enough to engulf and obliterate them. Their bodies rolled and pumped and finally imploded. She couldn't bare it, it was too much! She yelled out in passion and held onto Lee as his body guided them back down to reason. With one last bit of effort, Lee rolled off of her and onto his back before going limp.

Neither could talk but lay side by side panting, trying to catch their breaths. Tory's hand moved to his and she gently stroked his fingertips. He opened his hand and she traced his palm, moving across the cast before holding his hand tightly in hers.

"Tory Torres." He said.

She laughed. They were in the bath, much easier than trying to shower and keep his casts from getting wet. They made water casts but she guessed no one had stopped to think how much more convenient it would be for a person with two arms in a cast to keep them dry.

"Victoria Torres, Victoria das Torres, Tory das Torres," She tested the names and sighed happily. Her back was leaned against his front and his arms rested on the sides of the tub. "I love the sound of it, even though I sound like I'm a character in a Dr. Suess book."

"Mmmm, I want to be married to you Tory Torres; Mrs. Tory Torres." He kissed her temple.

"When?"

"Mmmm, up to you."

"Next week."

He laughed. "I have a huge family and they aren't all situated in Ohio. Three months? That will give us time to prepare."

She made a face. "I guess…" she wiggled her hips. "As long as we can keep pretending like we're married."

His fingers gently grazed her nipple. "I can agree to that."

"I think we really need to pick out rings."

"Mmmm," he sighed in contentment. "Whatever you want, *querida*, I want you to have. Oh yeah, I know that you aren't Catholic but I'd really like to get married in my church. Would that be okay?"

"Oh yes. I love your church." But it was huge. It sounded like he wanted a big wedding. She turned slightly to regard him. "We need to talk about finances."

"Yes we do." He sighed. "But let's get out of the bath. "My cock is getting wrinkly."

"Ooo bad boy," she laughed.

"Plus my parents will return soon and I'd rather not give their imagination fodder."

She wrapped a towel around herself and frowned. "You didn't make love to me last night."

He paused in drying off and then wrapped the towel around his waist. "Tory, I know just how much sound it takes to be heard in that other room…"

"Ah, gotcha."

"I'm an adult but the idea of my parents listening to us make love is…"

"Yeah, okay, yeah."

After they dressed and were comfortable in the living room, Lee got them iced tea and then she rested in his arms. She didn't know why this topic was so difficult for her; maybe because she didn't want to be impacted by the amount of money he made. If he was poor she would love him no less and if he was a millionaire she couldn't love him more than she did at this very moment.

"Tory, if I had my fondest wish, it would be for you to quit work and to allow me to take care of you financially."

She made a face. "But then you'd have to give me an allowance…"

"No. Why would you need an allowance for what is essentially ours? The only thing I'd ask is that if we make any major purchases we discuss it first. Other than that what's mine is yours; ours."

"Well…" she bit her lip. "I do have these student loans…"

"Tory, I make a hundred and twenty thousand a year without even trying. I can make double that just by transcribing more books. Visually impaired people are always going to want books, even in the digital age and there is never going to stop being books that people need transcribed. I have great benefits and my boss is also a personal friend of mine. We've been buddies since we met at the blind academy when we were both sixteen. When he started this company I was the first person he contacted and I've been with him for ages. So I'm in a secure job, my finances are secure and-"

"Okay," She grinned. "I'll quit my job. I really...hate that job."

He kissed her and seemed relieved. "I know you do. And it's not that I don't want you working. I just don't want you working at some job that you don't like and that doesn't appreciate you. I mean if you were doing something else that you liked; like how my sisters have their restaurant than I'd support that completely."

She considered his words. Would she want to start her own business? If she could do anything that her hearts desired, what would it be?

"I don't know what I'd want to do for a career, but I do know that I want to do something. If it's okay I'd like to find some type of job that I'd enjoy."

He nodded. "My only requirement is that you like whatever it is you chose to do."

She snuggled deeply into his arms. "I am quite possibly the luckiest woman in the world."

After church, Mr. and Mrs. Torres announced that they would return home the following day. Everybody objected but understood. Dinner was at Kaye and Paulo's big home where the entire family showed up to spend one last family dinner with the matriarch and patriarch of their large clan.

Rosalind was even present with her two boys Brice, jr and Michael. Tory was determined not to allow the other woman to get under her skin. Lee was so solidly hers that there was nothing Roz could do to change that.

In the kitchen, the ladies convened to prepare the meal. Tory knew what to do in the kitchen but since Mama Torres (Mrs. Torres insisted she stop with the MRS and call her Mama) was present all rolls were changed as the older woman took charge of making an authentic Azorean dinner. And to think, all this time she thought she was eating authentic Azorean food!

She was told to make *arroz doce* instead of the *aletria* that she usually made. And there would also be deep fried calamari as well as squid sautéed in olive oil and wine, grilled linguica, little neck clams, beer mussels, *caldo verde sopa,* and a braised beef served with potatoes and carrots called *carne guizada.* She liked being in the kitchen with Mama Torres, who seemed to know everything about cooking just by sight. She knew when Kaye needed to add more salt to the beef and that Francine's wine wouldn't do for the *molho vilao.*

"When will I be returning for the wedding?" Mama Torres asked with a sly smile.

Tory grinned as she stirred the custard. "Three months." Everyone began to whoop in excitement, everyone except for Roz who was pretending that Tory wasn't present.

"Have you picked out a ring?"

"Where is the wedding going to be held?"

"Where is the honeymoon?"

She giggled happily and held up her hands. "We haven't decided on all of that yet. The only thing we know is that we're going to be married in the church."

Rosalind's head whipped around. "But you're not even Catholic. Only Catholics can get married in a Catholic church. Everybody knows that."

"Nonsense," Kaye said. "Father Romano knows us like his second rib. He wouldn't want anybody else to do the nuptials."

Macey piped up. "And if he dared to raise a stink he'd lose all of us."

"That's right!" Everyone agreed, including Senna and Leticia, which surprised Tory. It appeared that the tides were turning back to her. Roz wisely kept her mouth shut.

While the men watched the big screen television in the other room, Mama Torres went off to spend time with the grand children. The women sat and had wine and cheese in the dining room.

"How are you holding up?" Leticia asked Rosalind. Rosalind shrugged and sighed. "I'm fine but the boys are having a difficult time. I'm happy they have all of their cousins here to play with, and of course their aunts and uncles."

Ugh, what cousins? What aunts and uncles? She wasn't even related to them, Tory thought as she hid a scowl.

Katy, who was married to Carlo patted the other woman's hand. "You have us, Roz, don't forget that."

"I appreciate that. My family is back home and you are all the family I have now."

Francie gave her hand a pat. "You'll always have us. God willing you will find the love that you deserve." Tory watched as Roz shrugged and looked down forlornly. She almost said, ugh, out loud at her fakeness.

"I don't think I want to be in love. I've had two great loves and both ended leaving me in misery." The room grew quiet. "If I could I would go back in time and choose wisely in my youth." She gave Tory a careful smile. "Then I'd be happily married just like the rest of you."

Fiona made a sound of disapproval at her words.

"Rosalind, watch your mouth."

"I don't mean any disrespect. These are just the words of a broken hearted woman." She stood. "Excuse me. I'm going to take *cerveja* to the men." Tory counted to ten...and then to twenty before she felt it was safe to stop gripping her chair handle so that she wouldn't jump down Roz's throat!

"Who invited her?" Macey muttered after a few quiet moments. Everyone chuckled.

At dinner Lee was having a tough time feeding himself because it was too difficult to cut the beef with the cast. Tory took great pleasure in feeding him and shushing him when he complained that he could do it. She delivered a kiss to his cheek to quiet his protests and then the men laughed and complimented him on figuring out how to be served so efficiently. Tory joined in the good-natured razing and despite the careful glares by Rosalind, Tory felt like everything between her and the Torres family had returned to normal.

During dessert, Rosalind commented that she would be willing to drive Lee and Tory home.

"We have our own car." Lee responded.

"I'm just offering because I noticed that Tory was drinking."

That was it! That was the last straw. "What are you trying to say?" Tory asked. "Are you suggesting that I'm not able to drive safely?"

"Not at all."

Paulo opened his mouth to make a joke but Kaye stopped him and so the room grew quiet.

"Accidents happen," Rosalind stated.

227

"Especially when others are driving down the wrong side of the street." Lee added.

"Yes," Raphael agreed with a chuckle. "That is usually a sure fire way to start an accident."

The tension lifted except between Rosalind and Tory who watched each other warily from across the table. For one split second, Tory thought about letting it get swept under the table. She thought about leading the rest of her and Lee's life together with her ignoring the other woman as she took pot shots at her. And in that moment she knew that she couldn't. She might be about to stick her foot in her mouth and mess everything up but she wouldn't go another second pretending.

"Rosalind," Tory said, cutting through the chatter. "Say what you've been dying to say all evening. I know you've been waiting for the best opportunity, so go ahead and get it off your chest."

"I have nothing to say. But you sound like there is something that you might want to get off your chest."

Kaye stood and ushered the young ones remaining at their seats around the card table to the other room to play video games.

"Rosalind, what are you doing?" Lee asked.

Papa Torres stopped Mama Torres from intervening and the older couple remained quiet along with the other members of the family.

"It's okay." Tory said. "I do want to talk to you all. I know that some of you have voiced a concern about what happened the night of the accident. I know some of you are worried that I might not be responsible enough to be married to a visually impaired man."

"Tory, you owe no one an explanation-" Lee began but she placed her hand on his.

"No honey, this needs to be said." She looked at everyone around the table. Macey gave her a look of approval. Tory allowed her eyes to rest on Rosalind. "I'm not going to meet a man that is visually impaired and just because I fall head over heels in love with him immediately know everything there is to know about his blindness. But Lee is a great teacher. He's taught me how to dance like I'm Portuguese, and how not to move the furniture. He's taught me how to accept...my shortcomings. I've taught him things too. I've taught him that his inability to see does not impact the love that a woman can have for him. Somehow I don't think he's learned that from...past relationships." Someone snickered and Rosalind's eyes flitted to that person.

"On the night of the accident, after we left the restaurant we walked to our car. We even stopped and kissed right there on the sidewalk." Lee took her hand. "I remember thinking that I was the luckiest woman in the world. We got into the car and he reached out and took my hand as I drove. I looked at him and thought, he looks the way I feel." Tory smiled to herself. "I never thought that I'd meet a man that could feel that way about me." Lee squeezed her hand.

"I don't know how long I looked at him; about as long as someone looks at their radio dial when they're changing the channel, or glances in the back seat at their sleeping child, or at their cell phone when they missed a call. And then I heard a horn blow and I looked up just in time to see that car right there in front of us. How long does it take a car driving thirty miles an hour to drive a few yards? How much time do you need to spend the wheel? I can't answer those questions. All I know is that I turned the wheel hard and fast...but it wasn't fast enough.

"So...there you have it. You decide what you need to decide. Lee and I have already talked about it and he knows how I feel. I'm going to always doubt myself because of that night. But I'm also always going to adapt and learn from my mistakes. More importantly, I'm never going to worry about how you or anyone else feels about me. Lee loves me and that is all I need to make me happy."

Rosalind looked around the table and then looked at Tory. "I know that you will be a good wife to Lee. You don't need to prove anything to anyone. I just hope that you and I can be friends-"

"No we can't. But we don't need to be enemies." Tory said flatly. *See bitch, I don't trust you and now everybody knows it. Game over!*

"Tory," Rosalind said quickly, "I'm not trying to interfere in your life! We all love Lee and just want the best for him-"

"Rosalind! *Cala-te praí!* This conversation is over! She doesn't want to be friends with you and that is it. For the rest of you, I need to tell you, that you are driving me NUTS! I can't freaking breathe without one of you calling or stopping by! I love you, but this has to end! Now, I know you worry but it's not needed."

There was some vocal disagreement and Lee argued back. Rosalind got up and left the table. She collected her boys and then left the house.

"Lee, I can't believe that you think that we can just turn off our love for you!" Francie stated.

"STOP IT!" Mr. Torres stood and slammed his fist on the table. "You children are worse than the ones playing in the other room!" He looked at Tory. "Please forgive us. You must think we're a crazy family."

She smiled. "A passionate family. A loving family...but yes, a little crazy, too."

There was a single chuckle and then another and before they knew it they were all laughing. Tory leaned her head against Lee's shoulders and held onto his arm. This was the crazy family that she desperately wanted to be a part of.

But if she was truly going to be a part of this family, she would need to learn to stop being so shy and to speak her mind. She smiled to herself. Somehow she thought that she would figure it out.

CHAPTER 18

When Monday rolled around Tory was happy to stretch in Lee's bed and to snicker at the alarm clock. She should throw it out the window! She contemplated rolling over and going back to sleep but she did have some business to take care of. Tory planted a kiss on Lee's lips, not waking him, and then she pulled on her robe and went into the other room to make a phone call.

She called her boss and told a little white lie. She said that due to her accident she would need to quit her job and that she was unable to give 2 weeks notice as she was still at home convalescing. She was surprised at the genuine sadness in her boss' voice.

"We'll miss you Victoria. You're a very hard worker. Take care of yourself and I'll be sure to have your final pay check mailed out to you."

"Thanks Harold. Sorry to leave you in a lurch." She felt bad, but not bad enough to go back to work. She checked the time and knew that Mama would be awake so she decided to call her next.

"Hi Mom."

"Hi, honey. How're you feeling?"

"So much better."

"That's good."

"Sorry that I'm just now getting back to you. The family had a going away dinner for Lee's parents. They're returning to the Azores."

"I like Lee's family. They're very nice and they all genuinely like you." Mama's words caused her to beam. "Have you been using the spirometer?"

"Uh..." Damn she didn't even have a lie prepared.

"Tory." Mom said firmly. "Taking care of yourself is very important. If you don't then you will have a set-back." She made a face. Making love with Lee was the only lung exercise she needed, but she couldn't say that to her mother.

"I'm going to use it."

Her mother paused. "Tory, I don't want to upset you, but I don't want this to turn into another situation like the last time."

The breath caught in Tory's throat and she was shocked into speechlessness that her mother would be bringing that up.

"You didn't take care of yourself and then things got out of hand."

"Mama, that's not fair." She whispered, squeezing her hand into a fist in her distress. "I was just 18. I was a kid-"

"Baby, I know. But you didn't go to the hospital until it was too late. Honey, it could have ended up being a pregnancy or HIV. You could

234

have lost your life instead of just an ovary to an untreated STD."

She didn't want to talk about this. She desperately tried to think of a way to end this conversation. She didn't want to go back there...

"It's just that everything was worse because you didn't take care of yourself and I just want to make sure that you do this time."

She nodded quickly. "Yeah I will."

"Tory..." her mother's voice softened. "Does Lee know about..."

"I told him-"

"Even about contracting Chlamydia and losing your fallopian tube to it?"

"Mama, I'll have to call you back!" Her stomach lurched and she dropped the phone and hurried to the bathroom where she became violently ill. Why did she have to bring that up? She had spent so much time trying to put that behind her only to have it brought up while she was so vulnerable. Thinking about that disease living in her body all of that time made her feel dirty again. She wasn't dirty the way that disease made it seem.

After being sick Tory turned on the shower and let the water run down her body, cleansing her, absolving her.

"Tory?" She jumped at the sound of Lee's voice. "You've been in there forever. Are you okay, honey?"

She turned off the water. "Yes, I'm coming out."

No. She was never going to tell Lee about this. Why should she? Guilt caused her to become cold and to begin to shiver uncontrollably as she dried herself. The answer to that question was obvious; because she only had one ovary and Lee wanted a houseful of children — and not just Lee, she wanted that too. But what if that fucking disease cost her the ability to have babies? No, not the disease, but her own ignorance because she hadn't wanted to face what had happened to her.

"Shall we go ring shopping today?" Lee asked as they sat at the table drinking coffee and eating danishes.

"What?"

Lee chuckled. "You are really out of it today. Are you feeling okay?"

"Yeah, I'm just...I quit my job this morning."

"Did they hassle you?"

"No, it actually went pretty smooth."

"Good. I wouldn't want to have to pay them a visit. I can do a lot of damage with my cane." Tory smiled and then reached for his hand and held it. "So, do you want to go ring shopping?"

She forced herself to put her past behind her where maybe she could bury it again. She smiled at her man. "Hell yeah! Let's go ring shopping!"

They found their rings that very day and were told that they would be ready for pick up in about a week. They scheduled their final doctor's appointment for the same day and then after the check up and the ring pick up, the plan was to visit the restaurant and show them off to the family. Lee had already called everyone to a gathering and Tory suspected that he was going to propose again but this time present her with the engagement ring. She was becoming spoiled at his attention because she wanted him to do it again and again.

Tory woke up that morning and coughed up phlegm into a tissue. She had developed a nagging cough that had begun as a tickle in the back of her throat but had gotten steadily worse as the week progressed. Now her chest ached from the constant coughing.

Lee rubbed her back as she coughed up a wad of mucus. "That sounds bad. We'll have the doctor write you a prescription for some cough medicine."

She sat there for a moment catching her breath and kicking herself for foregoing the spirometer. But she had been active and didn't think that it was that big of a deal. With a sigh she pulled herself to her feet and got ready for her day.

The first stop was the rings and they were perfect. Lee refused to give her the engagement ring and she giggled knowing that her earlier suspicions were probably right and he was going to present it to her in front of his family this evening. She noted the curious looks of the other patrons and forgot to wonder what they thought.

Tory drove them to the hospital, happy that it would be the last visit for the both of them until Lee had his casts removed. He was given a clean bill of health and then next it was her turn to get checked out. However her doctor wasn't nearly as pleased with her progress as Dr. Hendrix had been with Lee's.

"Well, I believe that you're developing pneumonia." He removed his glasses and regarded her with an intense stare. "Have you been using the incentive spirometer?"

Tory froze. Lee frowned and tilted his head. "What is an incentive spirometer?"

The doctor took a few moments to describe it to Lee and to explain its importance.

"So it's essential to her healing? Is that what you're saying?"

Tory winced as her doctor confirmed that it was. "We'll need to schedule a chest x-ray just to be sure. We better do a urinalysis and blood test first and that will determine the course of treatment." He sighed. "Young lady, I need for you to utilize that incentive spirometer as prescribed and to get some bed rest, because you and I discussed in great length your increased risk of stroke or heart attack. Okay?"

"Okay." She said, properly chastised. Why did he have to say all of that in front of Lee? Couldn't he have used some form of discretion? Lee remained quiet as the nurse gave her a cup to pee into and then sent her to get her blood work done.

When she returned to wait for the chest x-ray she took in Lee's stiff posture from his seat in the plastic office chair. He still hadn't said one word. Okay, so he was not happy with her right now.

"You're quiet." She said, attempting to thaw him out a bit.

"You lied to me," he said flatly.

Her mouth dropped. "Lee-" Lied? What?

"You don't get it, do you?"

"What?" Pain, brought on by his words caused her eyes to widen.

"I need you to be my eyes and that doesn't mean just telling me shit that you want me to know and not telling me shit that you don't! How do you think it makes me feel knowing that you were getting sicker and sicker and I didn't know why because you didn't tell me?"

"But-"

"No buts!" He scowled and came to his feet, pulling his cane from the pocket of his cargo pants. "Macey will pick me up. You go home, get that spirometer thing and you use it!" He walked out the door with lurching footsteps, tapping his cane loudly as he went.

"Lee!"

He ignored her and kept walking away. She watched him as the nurse returned with a file in her hands. She looked uncomfortable as she looked from Lee's disappearing form back to Tory.

"Uh...this might not be the right time but congratulations. You're pregnant."

CHAPTER 19

"We obviously can't give you a chest X-Ray but we can do a rapid urine and mucus test."

Tory was staring at the doctor stunned. She'd been sitting in her hard little chair for the last five minutes speechless. The doctor finally sighed. "Look, I understand that this is unexpected...and probably not happening at a good time. I'm sorry for anything I may have said...but your pregnancy adds a new spin to this. Your body hasn't healed from the accident. You have to take care of yourself. I cannot stress that enough. You can have a heart attack or stroke very easily."

She clutched her stomach protectively and nodded. "I promise. I'll use the spirometer-"

"And make an appointment with a prenatal doctor as soon as possible. The tests indicate that you are very early into your pregnancy and we need to make sure that you and your baby stay healthy." Tears stung her eyes. The doctor reached out and took her hand. Her baby...she could actually have a baby.

Tory suddenly realized something that shamed her as much as contracting the venereal disease had. She really had doubted her ability to have babies. And if she had not been able to get pregnant, would she have ever told Lee? She didn't know the answer to that and not knowing that about herself meant that Lee was pretty much correct in everything that he'd said to her. He'd said that she didn't get it…and she guessed he was right.

Tory spent hours at the hospital getting tested and treated for what turned out to be a mild case of pneumonia. Her doctor wanted to admit her in order to put her on an intravenous course of antibiotics but she begged him to allow her to go home. He met her half way and gave her a three hour I.V. and then released her. By that time it was well after six and she was nearly fit to be tied with anxiety and worry. In the hours that she'd had to sit and think while accepting the I.V. Tory replayed Lee's words, examining them from all angles and she came to a difficult realization.

She needed to tell him everything about her rape. Maybe he would think that she was dirty for having an STD; *the clap*, and living with it for months. It was a stigma that she couldn't live down, especially since her mother and father had to be told once she was emitted to emergency. What if Lee looked at her with the same shock, disappointment and disgust?

Tory stopped walking, suddenly feeling overwhelmed as her past and present came crashing together. She took a deep breath and placed her hand on her chest. That rape just kept happening over and over—even years later. She climbed into her darkened car and stared at nothing.

Tory thought about just going home, using the spirometer and falling into bed in exhaustion, but she couldn't allow Lee to go on being mad at her and she wanted to share the news about the baby. So she decided to drive to the restaurant figuring that Macy would have taken him there since the family was meeting for dinner. She thought about calling his cell phone first, just to make sure of his whereabouts, but couldn't bring herself to do it. The idea that he would lash out at her was just too much for her to bear right now. She knew that he wouldn't do that in front of his family...would he? Regardless, she was going to the restaurant because no matter what, she still needed to eat. She patted her tummy and felt a small grin tug at her lips. She had two to feed.

The street was lined with cars and it gave her a sense of déjà vu as she hurried to the restaurant. A chill ran down her spine and for a moment she thought about turning around and going back home. She was emotionally drained, but her desire to see Lee over ruled her good senses. She hurried into the restaurant and was relieved to see that the host for the night was not Roz but a young man. He recognized her and greeted her with a smile.

"They are all gathered at their family table."

She thanked him and then hurried through the room and searched for Lee. She saw him at the oversized table, having desert with his siblings.

Carlo's wife, Katy smiled when she saw her. "You came! Lee, Tory's here."

She saw a shadow fall across his face. Raphael, who was sitting next to his brother collected his place setting and moved so that she could sit down next to him. She greeted everyone in a distracted manner and sat down next to Lee.

"Lee said you were sick." Paulo said. "We wouldn't have eaten without you if we knew you were coming. Well there's still food. There's ALWAYS food," he joked.

"It's okay…" She glanced at Lee who said nothing.

Macy filled a plate with food and then passed it to her while Francie passed her a glass of wine.

"What are you doing here?" Lee finally asked.

She stared at him. "I was going to eat."

He sat there silently, not eating, speaking or moving. Tory's expression dropped. Rosalind sat across from them looking on with interest.

"How did your doctor's appointment go?" She had the nerves to ask.

Tory shot her a heated look. Why was this woman always around?! "Fine," was her simple response.

Lee reached for his glass of water and knocked it over. Tory jumped up and reached for a napkin and began cleaning the spill.

"Tory," he sighed. "Just...leave it."

"I almost got it-"

"Tory. Go home. Do what I told you to do."

The table grew instantly quiet. There was not a peep to be heard.

She blinked and stared at him in surprise. Her mouth opened but then closed. She dropped the napkin and slid her chair back and then rushed out of the room. Her face burned and her eyes stung. She heard Raphael exclaim that he should go after her and she heard his one word response.

No.

Tory choked back her tears and hurried to the car. She was just starting it when she heard someone call her name. She looked up sharply. Raphael was hurrying towards her.

"Tory!"

Reluctantly she rolled down the window and wiped her eyes. She just wanted to get out of here. She just wanted to go home and forget that she had just been dismissed by Lee in front of his family.

Raphael leaned down and gave her a concerned look. "Honey, what's wrong? I've never seen you two like this."

"We had a fight." She wiped her eyes and swallowed back a sob. Then she had a coughing fit and had to spit into a tissue.

He gave her a concerned frown. "Are you okay?" When she nodded he offered her a wry grin.

"Everyone does, you know. You'd be abnormal if you didn't."

She met his eyes. He was almost as handsome as his younger brother-darker, though, with glossy black hair, but the same facial features.

She looked down and then shook her head. "There's just…so much going on right now. I don't know, maybe he's getting tired of me."

Raphael chuckled. "No. That is not ever going to happen. My brother's life seems to revolve around your happiness." He gave Tory a sincere look. "He's angry about something but he will get over it Tory, okay?"

She chewed on her lower lip but then nodded her head. "Okay."

He stood back giving her space to drive away. "You drive safe. Go home and get some rest."

She managed a slight smile and then she pulled off and drove back to her home.

The most difficult thing about being in love with a blind man is remembering that his being blind is the least of it all. Being in love with a man that had his own individual thoughts, feelings and reactions was just as much of a consideration.

Tory rolled onto her side in her lonely bed and tried to sleep. She tossed and turned before falling into a restless sleep well after midnight.

The ringing of the telephone woke her up and she checked the time, 9 am. She reached for her cell phone and saw that it was Lee. Her heartbeat spiked but right before she was going to answer she put the phone back onto her bedside table. *Yeah, I'm chickening out.* But it was more than that, she was actually a little angry. His rejection last night had been devastating. She wasn't ready for an angry confrontation—not until she at least had gone to the bathroom.

She used the bathroom, brushed her teeth and then lifted up her nightshirt and stared at her stomach. Today she would make an appointment for a prenatal doctor. She had to be healthy because her life was no longer just her own. Too many people depended on her, including the man that she was currently pissed at.

With a sigh she returned to the bedroom and picked up the phone. It blinked that there was one message waiting. She accessed the voicemail and listened with her heart pounding in her chest.

"Tory…I'm sorry. I should never have yelled at you. You're sick and I'm acting like…I'm happy that my brother Ralph went after you but I'm sorry that it wasn't me. I want to come over. You need me to take care of you and I need to be with. I'm on my way."

She jumped up and looked around quickly. Shit! She needed to pick up around the room and to take a quick shower. She hurried around the room picking up clothes and shoes and tossing them into her closet. She thought about how Rosalind had called her house dirty--and it wasn't but it was untidy. She did a quick walk through of the small apartment, making sure that her parents hadn't moved anything. She made a few adjustments and then hurried to the shower. She was just finishing up when she heard Lee call her name.

"I'll be right out!" Tory grabbed her robe and quickly hurried into the living room where Lee was standing anxiously holding a paper sack.

"Uh…hi." She said.

"Hi." He held up the sack. "I brought donuts."

She took them from him and carried them to the kitchen. He followed. "How are you?"

"Uh...fine."

"Did you get my message?"

"Yeah." She placed the donuts on the kitchen counter and opened the refrigerator for the coffee. "Do you want coffee?"

"Why don't you get back into bed and I'll make the coffee. That's what I'm here for." She was prepared to object but decided not to. Walking past him to go back to the bedroom she noticed that he was carrying a pack. Was he moving in? He took it off and placed it in the corner and busied himself with the coffee preparation.

She climbed into bed and picked up the incentive spirometer and sucked on the mouthpiece watching the little ball move upward. She suddenly had a fit of coughing and spit into a tissue. Ugh

"Are you okay?" Lee called from the next room.

"Yeah. Just doing this lung exercise."

"Good. I'll be there in a minute." She rolled her eyes and then resumed her exercise. By the time he appeared carrying a tray with coffee and donuts she was finished and tired and a bit nauseous. She didn't really want the coffee or donuts. He carefully placed the tray on the bed and she picked it up and put it on her lap while he sat down on the bed facing her. She handed him his coffee and he thanked her and took a sip.

She politely handed him a donut, which he munched. And as she watched him she knew that it would be a lie to pretend that she wanted the coffee or donut.

"I'm not hungry."

He tilted his head. "Are you sure? You can have it later if you like."

"Okay."

He took the tray and carefully returned it to the kitchen. When he returned he just stood in the doorway quietly. "I am sorry."

"It's okay." She sighed.

"But I can't lie. I'm still angry."

She watched him. "Okay. I guess…maybe I am too."

Lee took a moment and then nodded. "I told you why I'm angry. I don't know what I've done to make you angry."

His calm voice was maddening.

"I'm not sure why I'm mad." She spoke in an equally calm voice.

He moved to the bed and sat down. "Tory, I need to know something and I need to know it right now."

She blew out a loud breath. "What?"

"Are you going to keep secrets from me?"

She shook her head. "Secrets?"

"Yes. If you're my extra set of eyes then I need to see what is real, not what you want me to see."

"God, I get that Lee. I'm sorry, okay! I didn't tell you about this stupid spirometer and it wasn't because I was trying to...conceal something from you. I just thought it was a stupid device that I didn't like using. God it wasn't a fucking conspiracy!" She climbed out of bed and slammed the covers down. She faced him again. "Look, I'm sorry. If you're asking me if I'll candy coat the bad shit then...no. I won't. But...did you have to call me a liar?"

He sighed. "I'm sorry. Yeah, you're right. It doesn't make you a liar. We just have to...understand each other."

"Well...you didn't have to just dismiss me in front of your family. That embarrassed me and I have to face them knowing that they saw me get 'put in my place'." She snapped. "Don't ever do that again, do you hear me? Don't ever talk to me like that in front of your family!"

He nodded and stood. "I'm so sorry. I was being childish and lashing out because..." he ran his hand through his hair in distress.

"Because you can't control the world? Earth to Lee; Even us sighted people can't." After a few moments he reached out and she gave him her hand. He pulled her towards him and hugged her.

"Tory...you deserve so much more than this. You should have someone who can-"

"Take care of me?"

He nodded.

She swallowed. "Would you rather..." She stepped out of his arms. "Would you rather be with someone like Rosalind?"

"Tory!"

"Someone who can anticipate your every need and who doesn't need to be taught how to care for you? Someone who would leave her husband so that she can be with you in the *right* way?"

"For the last time, I don't want Rosalind!"

"Good. For the last time, I don't want anyone but you. Got it?! I don't want a guy just because he can see! I don't want to be in love with anyone but you!"

He looked towards her quietly. His posture relaxed and then he shook his head and chuckled. "I'm nothing if I'm not tenacious in my insecurity."

She stepped back into his arms. "You have no reason to be insecure when it comes to me. I am completely and totally in love with you—even when I'm pissed off."

He nuzzled her temple. "So...I guess we can survive arguments."

"Yes, thankfully." She cleared her throat. "The question is, can we survive complete honesty?"

He stroked her hair. "It's what I need. I need to feel like you respect me enough to allow me to make my own decisions and I need to know that you won't control me with the information you give me. Tory I need to trust you completely, do you understand that?"

She nodded and squeezed her eyes closed. "Lee..."

"What, honey?"

"I didn't tell you everything about my rape." His hand paused in mid-stroke before resuming.

"Okay."

"I...I didn't go to the doctor or to the police immediately. I was so scared that I just went back to my dorm and huddled in my bed. As the months went on I began getting sick; back pain, nausea until finally...it got so bad that I went to emergency. There I was diagnosed with Chlamydia."

She felt him pause before he resumed stroking her hair.

"It had progressed so far that it caused PID, which is pelvic inflammatory disease." Lee stopped moving and tensed. "I...I lost one of my fallopian tubes to the disease. I had to call my parents and that is the only reason that they knew about the rape."

She heard him sigh and then he hugged her. "Did you think that I wouldn't love you anymore or that I would think less of you, *querida*?"

She shook her head. "I just know that this was something that I never wanted to share with anyone. And that has nothing to do with whether or not you can see. " She looked at him. "It was a...horrible part of my past and it wasn't something I wanted to relive." She felt tears in her eyes. "It doesn't make me feel...better for telling you that I contracted an STD. It makes me feel dirty and the fact that I lost an organ due to it makes me feel stupid on top of that." Angry frustrated tears streamed from her eyes and before she gave in fully to her tears, she tried to turn away. Only Lee's arms held her in place.

"Tory, Shh."

"I am not a dirty woman!"

"I know that honey." He cradled her in his strong arms while she cried out her shame against his shirt. "I don't think that at all. I just think that you were a scared kid that some dirty bastard took advantage of. My poor baby. You've been through so much." He kissed her tearstained face. "I just want to make you happy. That's all I want. I want to take care of you and I want to make sure that nothing ever hurts you again."

The tears ended and she allowed herself to luxuriate in her man's arms. "There's one more thing to tell you, okay?"

He paused and then stroked her back. "I think I know what you're going to say. And it's okay honey. We can adopt. There are so many options. I love you and nothing you tell me will ever change the way I feel about you. Do you understand?"

She took a deep breath. "Uh…yes. But that's not what I was going to tell you. You better sit down for this one."

His face was turning pale but he moved to the bed and sat down. She took his hands.

"Lee. We are going to have a baby."

His mouth dropped. "What?" He suddenly sounded like he was choking as he laughed out loud. "But…I don't understand. You were crying and talking about losing your fallopian tube and I thought you were going to tell me that we couldn't have a baby!" He jumped up and grabbed her into a tight hug. "But when did you find out?"

She was all smiles when he finally deposited her to her feet. "Yesterday when they took my urine they performed a pregnancy test. They couldn't give me an X-ray without it, I guess. Well…" She shrugged shyly. "It came back positive."

The smile froze on his face before completing dropping away. "You mean you found out yesterday? After I walked out?"

"Well…yeah."

He just shook his head, his expression was distressed and she frowned in confusion. "I can't believe that I walked out on you like that, Tory. I walked out while you were sick and while you were getting the news that you were having my baby." His voice grew thick with emotion and his eyes became suddenly bright as he stared at her. "Why in the fuck would you want me, Tory? I am a mess."

She sat down and pulled him down on the edge of the bed next to her and placed her head on his shoulder. "I can ask you the same thing, honey. Most men that would look at me would just see an overweight, under-employed college drop out...with a pretty face."

After a quiet moment he nudged her head with his. "Hey, stop talking about the mother of my baby like that. I happen to be very attracted to overweight, under-employed college dropouts with pretty faces."

They sat that way for a while, quiet, holding hands and thinking about how lucky they were to have each other.

"Tory..."

"Hmm?"

"I need to show you something."

She looked at him. He seemed worried. "What baby?"

"I need your computer."

She led him to the computer. She had the built in voice activation turned on so that he could use it to check his emails. He sat at her desk while she watched him peck away expertly.

"Is everything okay?" She asked.

He looked up at her. "Yes. I found this and when my parents were here I showed it to them. They really loved it and…I do too."

She watched the screen with a frown on her face. Suddenly it cleared when she saw what it was. A house. On Flores Island.

He waited tensely. "What do you think?" He finally asked. She threw her arms around his neck and hugged him tight. "I take that as a yes."

"I've listened to you talk about this Island paradise but I didn't think it would be possible to live there. I mean you have the job-"

"Which I can do anywhere."

"What about your brothers and sisters?"

"You know…they are kind of the incentive for this move. I kind of want to get away from them."

"You are joking?!"

"I am…but not entirely." He pulled her down into his lap. "I just want our children to have the freedom that I had. And maybe I believe in that saying; *Vou morrer pra minha terra* more than I thought."

I will die in my homeland.

She smiled and snuggled against his neck. "How big is this house?"

"Big enough for all ten of our kids."

CHAPTER 20

The next weekend dinner was held at Lee's loft. Lee had stayed several days at Tory's little apartment, making sure she got rest and used the spirometer--not that she needed his prompting. She had learned her lesson.

They decided that they would announce their intent to move and tell the family about the pregnancy during dinner. It wasn't easy to keep quiet. Every time she saw Macy, Tory would have a goofy smile on her face and was bursting to tell her.

Tory announced that she didn't need help cooking and it practically freaked everyone out. Dinner was already prepared by the time the family arrived; collard greens, smothered cabbage, roasted chicken with wild rice stuffing, macaroni and cheese, potato salad and corn pudding. Desert was a red velvet cake that she baked from scratch using her mother's recipe.

She found it humorous that the women just stood there with looks of uncertainty plastered across their faces because they had no tasks to accomplish--which was not the case with the men. The men gathered around Lee's computer and found something sports related to watch — chairs pulled from other areas of the loft. Soon they were happy in their own worlds.

Tory gave the kids some board games to choose from and some coloring books and crayons that she had picked up from the dollar store and once they were preoccupied she grinned at the ladies. Her grin was even broader because she had *not* invited Rosalind and didn't care if she felt snubbed!

"So ladies, sit down. I'm going to get wine for us and then I need your help." They looked at each other curiously as they sat on the couch, loveseat and some fold out chairs that Lee kept for just these occasions.

She brought out several bottles of wine, including some club soda for herself, and once everyone had glasses full she pulled out wedding catalogues. Now everyone was oohing an ahhing.

"Who needs a wedding planner when I have all of you for sisters?" She chuckled. By the time she called everyone to dinner they were so engrossed in planning the wedding that no one wanted to stop to eat. They had already determined the wedding day — barring some unforeseen event with the church. She had selected the style of wedding dress that she wanted as well as the style of bridesmaid dresses and a maid of honor dress for Macey who proudly accepted the role. Senna was going to set up appointments for cake tastings and Francie was already preparing the menu. Kaye offered to find a reception hall and Fiona and her daughters wanted to do the decorating. The bigger children then begged to help and of course Tory couldn't imagine not allowing them in on the fun.

When she finally managed to get everyone gathered around the table (two card tables pushed together for the youngsters), the sounds of eating stopped all conversation for a few long moments.

"Mmm." Tom, Senna's husband said. "I've never tasted cabbage this good before." Senna gave him a withering look before he looked down at his plate and continued eating quietly.

"So..." Senna asked while taking a second helping of cabbage. "How did you make this smothered cabbage?"

Dinner was a hit. Even the children ate everything on their plates. While dessert was being enjoyed, Tory and Lee couldn't stop the sappy smiles that appeared on their faces. They held hands looking like they were both cats that had caught the canaries.

Lee cleared his throat. "Everyone, thank you for coming."

"Let's thank Tory for making fifty pounds of delicious collard greens!" Raphael announced.

"You're welcome, Ralph," she giggled.

Lee took a deep breath. "Tory and I decided that after the wedding we're going to move to Flores." Someone gasped, and then everyone began speaking over each other in both Portuguese as well as English.

"English, please." Lee stated.

"Why?" Francie asked. "Why can't you wait a few years? We're just starting to know our new sister and now you want to take her away from us!"

"Uncle Lee, it won't be the same without you here!"

"You can't leave now, Lee!"

He held up his hands grimly. "I don't want to lose you guys, either. But if you think about it, Flores would be a wonderful place to raise that baby that is in Tory's belly, as well as all of the other ones that we plan to create. So you see-"

Someone screeched in joy and then suddenly everyone had left their seats to hug and kiss the couple.

Ten sets of hands touched Tory's belly although she didn't want to say that the roundness there wasn't due to a baby bump. In light of this new information there was a change of heart.

The baby would be Portuguese and that was that. The parents had no say. It would be born on Flores and then they could return to the states at a later date. It was settled. Tory and Lee just hugged and grinned. Whatever; as long as the arguing had stopped.

Someone turned on music and it was loud and then the dancing began. Lee pulled Tory into the center of the dancing bodies and despite his casts, he spun her, dipped her and then slapped her rear causing her and everyone else to roar with laughter. Then he made her sit down with water and she tapped her feet and clapped her hands and watched her brothers, sisters, nieces and nephews party late into the night.

The ringing of the telephone pulled the couple from their slumber early the next morning. It was Lee's cell phone that was ringing. He reached over sleepily and felt for it.

"What time is it?" He asked Tory.

She squinted at the bedside clock. "7:22 am." She saw a frown cross his face. "Hello?" He sat up suddenly. "What?"

Tory's heart began to speed up. "What is it, baby?"

"That is not a good idea…" He glanced at Tory and then covered the mouthpiece. "It's Rosalind. She wants to come over."

"What?!"

"Roz, it's early, we're still half asleep-"

"Give me that phone!" She snatched it out of his hands. "What do you want?! Why are you calling?"

Rosalind was crying. "So you won. You got knocked up! But if you hadn't pulled that then I would have gotten him. Just understand this, Lee and I have a special bond. We were each other's first! We made plans for a life together! Maybe not this second but soon he will see you for the stupid black cow that you are!"

Tory handed the phone back to Lee and watched as he listened silently to Rosalind's rant.

"I don't know why I thought that we could remain friends. Maybe because I remember that I used to love a girl that had the sound of laughter in her voice."

"Lee! Wait-" Rosalind tried to interject.

"You reminded me of the sea. Even when we came to the states I always felt like I was close to the sea whenever you were around...but you aren't that person anymore."

"Lee! I love you! I've finally admitted it to myself and now I can say it to you! I am in love with you and I can be everything that you need. You don't have to marry her! "

"Rosalind, it's not *just* that I don't love you. It's that I don't *want* to be in love with you. If there was no Tory I *still* wouldn't want you! You have been sneaky and conniving, telling me at the hospital how sorry you were that Tory and you had gotten off on the wrong foot, when all along you were just trying to turn my family against her. I don't trust you!" There was finally quiet on the other end of the line. "I never thought I'd say this, but you brought it on yourself. You and I can't be friends. I don't want to be friends with you. You stay away. If you come around, I won't be so kind." He disconnected the call and placed it on the bedside table.

He blew out a long, stressed breath. "I am so sorry about that. You should have never had to deal with the likes of her. I'm putting the word out that other than at the restaurant, she is not welcomed around me, you or our children."

Tory smiled. "Thank you." She hugged him.

Tory stood back and watched how Mama Torres expertly pulled the pot from the hot spring, which she had used to cook the *sopa* that Tory had prepared. The spring bubbled and steamed and Mama warned her for the millionth time to be careful even though she was a foot behind her. People were known to fall in, she cautioned. Tory knew that she was concerned because her stomach was huge and everything about her was now awkward. But she wasn't a weeble wobble toy! Sheesh. Still, Tory welcomed Mama Torres' lessons on how to be a true Azorean.

She and Lee had finally gotten settled in to their new home on the Island of Flores, and it had only taken about a month. All of the packages were unpacked—a necessity so that Lee could get his bearings in the new home. They had to ditch most of the furniture; shipping it would have cost a small fortune. The house was big and sparse; yet they didn't need much. Lee had joked that they would fill it with kids soon enough.

The first thing Tory realized upon landing on the island is that there were miles and miles of lush green hills and valleys, and the most beautiful flowers in every direction that you looked. And yet despite this, it was also a cultivated community. There were shops, restaurants, and events just like any other town. There were even tourists carrying around cameras and fanny packs! She did not feel out of place at all.

Mama and Papa Torres immediately took her under their wings and drove her and Lee all over, proudly showing off points of interest. She saw the waterfalls of Ribeira Grande, the Flores nature park, and the seat of the municipal government; Lajes das Flores, where Lee's parents lived. Tory and Lee's house was situated in a much smaller province called Faja Grande.

Their beautiful house was nestled at the bottom of a seaside cliff. The Ribeira Grande river was in plain sight, as was the sea — which meant so was the beach! Tory actually looked on in disbelief that something this beautiful could be all hers to enjoy. Lee proclaimed that the surfing was great here and promised to show her how after the baby was born. She gave him a quick look but he wasn't kidding. Damn, this man would never stop amazing her.

She was becoming well acclimated to island life. No more frantic bus rides to a horrible job, she no longer ate alone wishing to experience new and exotic foods, but best of all she had the man of her dreams who didn't consider her weight to be a negative — quite the opposite. And even though there were still days when he sometimes thought that she deserved someone better, and she still sometimes wondered why he loved her of all people, those times were becoming fewer and fewer.

She settled back in her seat in Mama Torres' 4-Runner and marveled at the scene unfolding before her. She counted another waterfall; that was three! Mama Torres spoke in slow Portuguese as they drove back to her and Lee's house. The other woman pointed out interesting sites and spoke proudly about her Island. Tory was getting good at picking up on what was being said even if she didn't always use the right tense or place words in the correct order when she tried to speak the foreign language.

When they arrived home, Mrs. Torres insisted on carrying the pot of *sopa*. Lee was on the sun porch behind his computer transcribing a new book. He was pushing out the books like crazy. He said the sun and sea breeze kept him invigorated and had turned the enclosed porch into his office.

He greeted them in Portuguese and ambled into the kitchen for a sampling of the soup before dinner. Mama smacked his hand and shooed him away and then gave them both big kisses and left to tend to her own dinner. Tory promptly removed the lid from the soup and gave Lee a sample.

"Almost as good as Mama's," he said in Portuguese. She had asked him to speak it as much as possible. She wanted to learn as quickly as she could and this was the best way for her to do it.

"Cooking Mama good taste," She said in choppy Portuguese. He smiled and pulled her to him for a kiss and then corrected the wording.

"Okay, we're going to do some exercise in translation." He said. She struggled to understand and then said yes. He slipped his hands beneath her blouse and sought her thick nipples beneath her bra.

"What are these big beautiful things I'm holding in my hands?"

She gasped and giggled and then squirmed away. "Bad." She said simply. "You're bad."

But then from across the room he heard her say, "*Chega cá...*"

He grinned and did as she requested; he went to her. She tossed her blouse at him and he caught it. She tossed her bra and he caught that as well. Tory shook her head. He still never ceased to amaze her.

When he was right in front of her, his arm snaked out and went around her waist. Then he kissed her, pulling her taut against his body as one arm clutched at her ample rear end and the other covered her swollen breast. He groaned deep in his throat as he dipped his head to capture her sweet nipple.

She sighed and closed her eyes as he gently pulled, sucking and using his tongue to flick and tease.

"Oh my God..." she groaned.

He peeked up at her, "*Meu Deus,*" he corrected. "*Meu Deus!*"

He swooped down and lifted her, her legs went around him swiftly despite an oversized belly between them. He walked them sure-footedly through the kitchen, living room and then up the stairs to their bedroom.

He placed her carefully on the bed and then slowly stripped out of his clothes. Tory watched him through lust slit eyes. It was like watching her own private stripper. *I must be the luckiest woman in the world...*

The End

They Say Love is Blind

PEPPER PACE BOOKS

STRANDED!
Juicy
Love Intertwined Vol. 1
Love Intertwined Vol. 2
Urban Vampire; The Turning
Urban Vampire; Creature of the Night
Urban Vampire; The Return of Alexis
Wheels of Steel Book 1
Wheels of Steel Book 2
Wheels of Steel Book 3
Angel Over My Shoulder
CRASH
Miscegenist Sabishii
They Say Love Is Blind
Beast
A Seal Upon Your Heart
Everything is Everything Book 1
Everything is Everything Book 2
Adaptation
About Coco's Room

SHORT STORIES
~~***~~

Someone to Love
The Way Home
MILF
Blair and the Emoboy
Emoboy the Submissive Dom

They Say Love is Blind

My Special Friend
Baby Girl and the Mean Boss
A Wrong Turn Towards Love
The Delicate Sadness
1-900-BrownSugar

COLLABORATIONS
~~***~~
Seduction: An Interracial Romance Anthology Vol.
1
Scandalous Heroes Box set

ABOUT THE AUTHOR

Pepper Pace creates a unique brand of Interracial/multicultural erotic romance. While her stories span the gamut from humorous to heartfelt, the common theme is crossing racial boundaries.

The author is comfortable in dealing with situations that are, at times, considered taboo. Readers find themselves questioning their own sense of right and wrong, attraction and desire. The author believes that an erotic romance should first begin with romance and only then does she offers a look behind the closed doors to the passion.

Pepper Pace lives in Cincinnati, Ohio where many of her stories take place. She writes in the genres of science fiction, youth, horror, urban lit and poetry. She is a member of several online role-playing groups and hosts several blogs. In addition to writing, the author is also an artist, an introverted recluse, a self proclaimed empath and a foodie. Pepper Pace can be contacted at her blog, Writing Feedback:

http://pepperpacefeedback.blogspot.com/

PepperPace.tumblr.com pepperpace.author@yahoo.com

AWARDS

Pepper Pace is a best selling author on Amazon and AllRomance e-books as well as Literotica.com. She is the winner of the 11th Annual Literotica Awards for 2009 for Best Reluctance story, as well as best Novels/Novella. She is also recipient of Literotica's August 2009 People's Choice Award, and was awarded second place in the January 2010 People's Choice Award. In the 12th Annual Literotica Awards for 2010, Pepper Pace won number one writer in the category of Novels/Novella as well as best interracial story. Pepper has also made notable accomplishments at Amazon. In 2013 she twice made the list of top 100 Erotic Authors and has reached the top 10 best sellers in multiple genres as well as placing in the semi-finals in the 2013 Amazon Breakthrough Author's contest.

40617946R00164

Made in the USA
Lexington, KY
13 April 2015